Ashfall Apocalypse

An Apocalyptic Thriller

M.L. Banner

Toes in the Water Publishing, LLC

Ashfall Apocalypse - Book #1 is an original work of fiction. The characters and dialogs are the products of this author's vivid imagination. Most of the science and the historical incidents described in this novel are based on reality, and so are its warnings.

PROLOGUE

Ron

'm so screwed!

That was my first thought, just before the massive wall of water hit me.

There was nothing selfless or noble going through my head at that moment, such as How is my wife? or even How do I save some of the people around me?

Sure, the heroes you read about in books or watched in movies would have no doubt done or thought something different. In real life, I guarantee any one of those fabled men or women would lose all thoughts of nobility if they had to stare down a million-trillion tons of water as I did.

But it wasn't my only ignoble thought.

In one of the frozen moments before the wave struck, it occurred to me, Oh crap, my iPhone is about to get wet. I had just bought the damned thing and now it was going to be ruined from all of this water.

Really, these were the only two thoughts that rifled through my mind a split-millisecond before the wall of water consumed me and every other living soul in that restaurant, and around our little town.

Time then stretched out like a long rubber band.

I know you've probably heard many of these stories from others, since the Big Death took out America. You've surely experienced it yourself. I think it's when something so quick and deadly strikes, it causes the world around you to appear to slow down to a crawl. Then it's like those few moments of horror are stretched out so that your mind can witness every part of that moment you would have otherwise missed... Just before cruel reality lets go of the stretched-out rubber band of horror, and it painfully snaps back at you.

But during that time stretch, you're also emotionally detached—the psychologists probably call it shock—so that you can deal with everything going on around you in your adrenalin-fueled state. At least that's what I thought in the early days, just after this happened.

Now, thinking more about that stretched-out moment in time, I realize it's more likely all that input pounding away at your senses has overwhelmed your brain, which is desperately trying to catch up and process it. All of those seemingly disconnected parts of that stretched-out moment are so damned vivid.

Even still today.

I remember the sharp aroma of the coffee, just sweetened by vanilla creamer, wafting up to my nostrils from the coffee shop's over-sized cup; the screams from those inside the shop and outside, with me, the loudest coming from Nanette, a stranger I'd just met and who was trying to work her way closer to me; the coldness of the dank blanket of wetness that at once enveloped me and then pummeled me backward; even the taste of the water was vivid—it tasted like dirty street, as in all the dirt and debris the monster wave must have scraped up from the street's surface just one millisecond earlier.

The last thing I remember before darkness consumed everything, and I tumbled for an immeasurable amount of time, was the sight of my wife's VW being washed toward me. Liz was inside stiff-clutching the steering wheel, eyes bulging wide with the knowledge that death was about to take her...

But I'm getting ahead of myself. Let me start with what led up to that moment, and then what brought us here.

CHAPTER 1

Ron

The world ended quietly for us like snowflakes... Gray snowflakes.

"Ron!" Liz's scream came from outside our house. "Come here quick."

I ran, rocketing through the front door, thinking she had fallen or it was a burglar, or something else that had to be bad.

Liz was standing outside, head tilted to the sky, mesmerized.

And then so was I.

Usually, where we lived, the weather was beautiful this time of year. Though, as you know, by that day nothing had been usual.

I was pretty ambivalent about the world around us. I had heard about the East Coast tsunami, and even the later damage to Corpus Christi, our closest coastal city. But I didn't really pay attention to it because it didn't immediately affect us. Weren't we all just focused on our daily lives, and nothing else?

By that time, I think we were just so numb to bad news and bad weather around the world. Liz and I had just ignored it.

Our own weather was all that mattered to me, as that affected my business and our Saturdays. And our weather had been rough days before. Weirdly rough. Now, looking back, it should have been obvious something bad was coming, or had already arrived.

It wasn't that we were unaccustomed to having bad weather. After all, we did have the occasional hurricane brush past us. Never a direct hit, but close enough to cause some wind damage and dump a shit-ton of water on us before moving on to the next place.

This was different.

Usually, the heat of summer started to introduce itself to us around this time of year. Not that it ever got too cold. The normal temperatures were pretty much as expected in the twenty-something years I had lived in this mostly tourist community: warm to hot, every day, with the rare exception of some cool mornings in the winter. Then a few days prior to that day, the weather turned violent.

First, eerie gray clouds rolled in like giant looming waves that covered the farthest reaches of the sky. But they yielded little to no rain, just lightning. Lots and lots of lightning, for hours at a time. One storm caused so many strikes near our house, a neighbor's home caught fire and burned to the ground. When we ran out to help, we noticed other fires in and around our town. Then, just as quickly as it started, the lightning stopped. That's when it started to get cold.

Temperatures dipped below freezing for the first time in memory, and it certainly never happened around this time of year. Then to punctuate the absurdity of it all, it snowed. Yet even the snow wasn't normal.

No, it wasn't the fairytale white stuff you'd see in Christmas movies, filling up ski slopes, skating rinks, and valleys. This stuff was gray.

It was what my wife had called me out to see. But it wasn't just Liz. Everyone, and I mean everyone, from our neighborhood had wandered outside their homes to gape at this gray stuff coming down and piling up in our yards and streets.

This was our warning sign of what was coming. Although even looking back at it now, I wonder what, if anything, we would have done differently.

So there I was, watching this gray snow accumulate on my outstretched palms, standing there like some half-frozen totem in our front yard. The snow felt cold, but there was something odd about it, besides its dirty color. I rubbed some of it against my forefinger and thumb and felt a sting. It was more abrasive than icy snow.

"You ever seen something like this before, Ron?" drawled my elderly next-door neighbor, who startled me from behind.

"Never. And it stinks," I said, finally acknowledging him. I saw my wife was chatting a few feet away with Bob's wife, Sarah.

"That's sulfur. And notice the abrasive quality of the snowflakes? It's frozen ash from a volcano," Bob said. His eyes were his usual red and watery. At least he was normal.

I chuckled a little at his words, because they hit me funny. "If volcanoes are hot, how could you have frozen ash?" My words came out stupid the moment they left my mouth. And like the seemingly never-ending snowfall, I tossed out another flurry of stupid. "Besides, last time I checked, we don't have many volcanoes in Texas, Bob."

"Ohhh," Bob stated as if he were waiting for my comment, "you probably didn't know, then, that volcanoes can shoot ash high into the atmosphere where the jet streams can take the ash cloud and move it halfway around the world at nearly the speed of sound. Then the weight of the ice crystals that form around the ash cause them to drop. These"—he shot his arms out and up to the sky—"are most likely from Mt. Erebus, in Antarctica, which started erupting last week."

"Well, that explains a lot of things, including the weird weather," I stated, probably in a vain attempt to erase some of my previous stupidity from our conversation. Though I wasn't done.

I hesitated, first looking up to the sky, and then over to my wife, and then I shot a sidelong glance at the other neighbors congregated on our cul-de-sac and in their yards around us.

All of us were being exposed to this strange phenomena. I pondered its abrasive quality and where it came from. "Are we safe out here... you know, with all of this stuff?"

"It's not radioactive or anything, Ron. No, you and your wife are safe."

Bob had a way of making me feel like an idiot most of the time, even when I wasn't making his job easier. I think he liked to torment me because he loved science and I was ambivalent about the physics of why things did what they did. I knew how things worked, just not the why, nor did I even care to find out.

But at that moment I wished I had paid more attention in my science classes. I wished I had read up on how everything fit together in the geological big picture so I would know what was going on, like Bob did. My life was focused on the small but functional: how a piston could be made to work smoothly, or how to Gerry-rig our boat hitch so that it stopped bouncing out of its cradle, or so many other things which just came naturally to me, without much thought.

"Later though," Bob drawled, "this will cause problems for engines, HVAC systems, and maybe even breathing..."

I was transfixed by the falling gray snow, listening to Bob lay out what this might mean, and the feeling that something was very wrong grew to the point of breaking.

I didn't know why; it felt foolish. But I couldn't help but feel that if I didn't get inside at that moment, I would somehow be closer to death. Maybe it was a premonition of what was to come. I don't know. I was simply certain we had to get under cover. Now.

"Thanks for the info, Bob," I hollered and gathered Liz by the hand, waving at him and his wife as we headed to our front door.

I whispered to Liz, "Do you remember hearing anything about volcanoes lately?"

We stepped back into the relative safety of our home.

"Only what Sarah told me about a huge eruption in the Antarctic, and one in the Atlantic. Why?"

I really don't remember what I said after that.
The next day, the rain started, volumes of it.

CHAPTER 2

Nan

This is about the time my life ended.

It had been pouring outside for a couple of days straight. I left work early, trying to beat my husband home and surprise him. I had just gotten a raise and that meant we could get the new truck he really wanted. I couldn't wait to tell him.

I was already soaked to the bone when I ran across the street and attempted to avoid the water jetting off the roofs above. I was mid-step when I was literally thrown to the ground, where I landed on all fours in a lake-sized puddle. The ground beneath me rumbled; the puddle surrounding me splashed up; the buildings in front of me appeared to move. I was terrified, but I've ridden a bucking horse before, and so I knew to hold on and wait.

Then the rumbling stopped, just as suddenly as it started.

I held there in that position, panting like a dog, and probably looking like one too.

There was an unending drumbeat of raindrops all around and the muffled sounds of car alarms hollering in the distance. Still, I listened for the rumble to begin again.

When I was sure it was over, I finally pushed myself up from the ground. But I held up where I stood, my legs somewhat wobbly, not caring about the rain at that point; I could not have been any wetter. But I was much more terrified that the earthquake would return, or that I was just imagining it was over. I'd never been outside of Texas, other than Juarez, Mexico for a day. So earthquakes were as foreign to me as... Well, snow; at least they were back then.

The urge to get home became overwhelming. I wanted to see what they said about the earthquake on television. My phone was dead, otherwise I would have checked on Twitter, like I had constantly done every moment with the tsunami damage back East and then along the Gulf Coast.

I moved one leg forward and my knee screamed back at me. My favorite slacks were torn and both knees were bleeding.

Some of the choicest words ever to come out of my mouth spilled from me at that moment. If I were a praying person, like so many were in our community, I'd probably have to ask for forgiveness for days because of what came out of my trap. It even embarrassed me to hear these words.

Feeling cleansed and ignoring the pain, I moved forward, first slowly, then running. The need to get back to our apartment turned into desperation, having already completely forgotten about my own news. I had to find out about what had just happened.

That's when my world ended.

Music assaulted my ears from our apartment the moment I opened our front door. This was odd, because I rarely listened to music and neither did Bud. So it wasn't likely that either of us would have left the radio on. And again, my husband shouldn't have been at home yet from his new job at the auto dealership.

Halfway inside, just above the blaring music, I could hear the laughter coming from our bedroom. Unconsciously, I closed the front door lightly and started to make my way to our bedroom. My conscious mind couldn't conceive of what was going on. Though deep down, I must have known.

That's when some naked nymph of a young dirty-blonde woman burst out of our bedroom, laughing in a high-pitched voice. She was moving toward me, while glancing back from where she had come, not watching where she was going. My husband taunted from the bedroom, "I'm coming to get you, Barbara."

It was this stupid shtick he did, mimicking that scene from Night of the Living Dead. He had done it to me the first time we had sex. And now he was doing it to this woman, who looked barely out of high school—far too young to have even known about the movie.

The young woman turned her head forward, whipping her long locks around, and she now glared in my direction. She hit a dead stop a few feet front of me, like she had slammed into a wall. Only her breasts moved, continuing to jiggle like two giant Jell-O molds. They came to rest, just as her face fell. "Oh hi, Mrs. Thompson."

It was Chloe from the auto dealership, where Bud worked detailing used cars and trucks. Chloe was the cute little receptionist who greeted everyone as they came into the dealership. And now that little tart was banging my husband. In our bed!

Bud blasted out of the bedroom, but halted at the door upon seeing me. His Johnson—that's what he called it—was standing at attention, like a private at roll-call. The giant shit-eating-grin he'd been wearing slid right off his face. "Nan-baby... Ah, this is not what it looks like."

Why do men say this? Really, do they think we are so stupid to accept this line of reasoning. Or is it that they are that stupid?

I glared at Bud and then at Chloe, as they stood like two naked statues, erect—although less and less by the second—and remaining in their places, completely mortified, waiting for my reaction. Any reaction.

I started to laugh.

It came out all at once, as torrential as the rainfall outside. I just howled like what I was looking at and what I had just heard was the funniest thing ever. And at the time, it was hilarious that the man I had been married to for ten-fricking-years was obviously carrying on with a teenager from work and when I caught him in the act, he said, "It's not what it looks like."

I continued to watch them as the unstoppable laughter emptied out of me. Chloe glanced back at Bud, whose own expression turned from shock to anger, as if I was the one at fault here: for coming home early, or for laughing at him, or for being amused by his now-flaccid Johnson or his little tart.

Chloe was the only one who seemed to have some sense of the situation. She quickly dashed to the living room, collected her clothes which were strewn around the floor, and then darted into the guest bathroom. She knew exactly where it was. This is when my laughter turned into rage.

When I returned my glare to Bud, he had decided to do something similar. I caught a flash of his hairy backside as he flew into our bedroom, threw on jeans and a shirt, which he was buttoning up while walking toward me, flashing his best car-salesman-like-smile. "Let me explain—"

I thrust out my hand, palm extended, cutting him off. If he said another word, I really felt like I would have leapt at him and scratched his eyes out.

At the same time, Chloe dashed out of the bathroom door, fully dressed in a tight blouse and mini-skirt, and slid through the partially opened front door.

"Wait!" Bud yelled, stopping her at the threshold.

Finally I spoke, choking back my anger. "You better go with her, because I don't ever want to see you in this apartment again." There was no more laughter in my voice.

His mouth opened, like he was going to tell me another lie. Then he thought better of it, snapping it shut. He looked around, found his shoes, slipped them on as he pushed his phone into his front pocket. "Can I, Clo?" he pleaded in a soft voice.

Chloe nodded.

As I watched him trudge out of our apartment, he shot me a reticent glance that flashed an "I'm sorry," but even he knew he didn't mean it. Then he slammed the door behind him.

The Spice Girls sang out, "Tell me what you want; what you really-really want—"

I ripped the offending clock radio out of the wall and threw it at the ridiculous picture of the cowboy roping a blonde cowgirl, hanging on the other side of our living room—a present from that miserable husband of mine. The silenced clock radio crashed against the picture, shattering its glass and knocking the whole monstrosity down onto the floor. A perfect representation of our marriage: shattered bits of useless garbage, lying in a heap.

I stood there in complete and utter shock, dripping blood and water onto our cheap apartment floors, when I heard voices from the bedroom TV...

"The 6.9 earthquake's epicenter was in Galveston, but it was felt all over Texas. It's just one more strange event attributed to the multi-volcanic eruptions throughout the Antarctic and elsewhere. We go now to Ashley Brown in Fort Worth."

CHAPTER 3

Ron

T hen came our Last Saturday.

We would have normally met the day with great excitement. Each Saturday, my wife and I would pack up the truck and boat and drive to the lake, where we would hang out on the water, fish, or anchor off a beach. Boat days were something that Liz and I coveted. It was our time alone. We would talk or fish and just enjoy each other. We just loved the water. It was our solace from this crazy world. The rule was, if neither of us had work we had to do, we headed to the water together and soaked up the sun. And because of where we lived—it was almost always sunny— Saturdays were truly our days.

At least they were.

Unfortunately, this day was way too wet and gloomy to be outside. So Liz went to work at her tax office and I played around in the shop all day. Later, Liz called and said that she wanted to meet me for dinner; neither of us felt like cooking, and it had been a while since we went out. I told her I was cold, and the shop's coffee maker finally gave up the ghost—apparently it didn't like the rain either. So I suggested we meet at our favorite coffee shop and then we'd go to the restaurant next door and enjoy a meal together. That would be our Saturday.

At the coffee shop, I grabbed a giant regular coffee, with lots of French Vanilla creamer—what can I say, I love my coffee frou-frou'd up—and headed outside. There were tables under a covered patio area, where I could see my wife pull up. I had assumed I would be the only one out there, because the weather was truly deplorable: It was breezy and there was that cold wetness that seeped into your bones, even when you weren't directly in the rain.

To my amazement, when I pushed through the door leading to that area, there were others outside as well. All appeared to be mesmerized by the torrential downpour beyond the cloth and plastic shelter. Some were staring at their phones.

There was chatter all around the tables about the earthquake. Some said there were multiple earthquakes, but I had only felt the one a few days earlier. And it really wasn't that big, maybe a five-point-five. As I was originally from California, what we had experienced was a fairly common occurrence there. But it wasn't just the common need to talk about the earthquakes, distant volcanoes and the torrential rains which drew every patron's attention, including my own, that night.

Unseen within the eerie darkness was a constant but growing rumble in the heavens. Add this to the odd torrential rainfall and previous events...

It made it seem almost—

"Apocalyptic, isn't it?" asked a female voice from behind me. I turned to see a pretty woman wearing a big grin, like she knew me, approaching me.

"I'm sorry, what did you say?" I asked. I didn't recognize her but thought she must have known me from somewhere in town and I didn't want to be rude.

"It almost looks like some sort of Biblical apocalypse is going on right before us, doesn't it?" She tossed me a bedroom smile and shot me a flirtatious glance with two of the most jarring blue eyes I had ever seen.

I had had the same thought (about the apocalyptic storm outside), which was mostly why I didn't answer her right away. But it was also her whole flirtatious persona that just knocked me off center.

"Cat got your tongue?" She giggled.

"Ah, yeah," I stuttered, though I'm not sure why. For some reason, her words, or her presence was completely disarming to me. Women didn't flirt with me too much, and I went out of my way to not do the same.

"So the cat did get your tongue?" She grinned wider this time, while combing back a short lock of her hair to an ear.

"Ah, no! I mean, yes, it does look like some sort of apocalypse," I spat out.

"Hi, I'm Nanette, but you can call me Nan. Everyone else does." She stuck out a delicate hand.

I accepted and shook lightly. Her fingers were cold and soft. "Ronald."

"Pleasure to meet you, Ron." She squeezed like a little vise and pumped my hand up and down. She didn't let go. Her eyes remained uncomfortably locked onto mine, like she was fishing for something inside me.

And I guess I must have been gazing back at her.

She swallowed, glanced down and then up again with another flirtatious flutter of her eyes, and said, "You know you could have me, if you asked." Her voice was a little tentative and yet casual, like she were asking me to pass the sugar.

I gulped.

Then a sudden burst of panic hit and that's when everything inside of me yelled, Get the hell out of here, Ronald. It was one thing when a woman was coming on to me. But Nanette had complete missile-lock.

She remained clasped onto my hand. I was shocked to realize I hadn't yet let go of her either.

I yanked my hand away and purposely grabbed my coffee with my other: my overt attempt to brandish my wedding band, holding it out in front of her to see, like some shield.

"Don't worry, I won't tell her about us, if you don't."

Aw, shit, I thought. Time to nip this in the bud.

"Look Nanette—"

"—Please call me Nan."

"Fine, Nan. You're very pretty and all—"

"Bet you say that to all the women who hit on you."

"Ah, look..." I was stammering so bad, and I was practically hyperventilating. Chill Ronald, chill, I told myself. "Were I single, I—"

"—you're single and yet you wear a wedding ri—"

"Stop! Thanks, but I'm here waiting for my wife. So please go away."

It was as if I had slapped her. Her mouth fell agape, and her eyes went wide, like she was in utter disbelief at my rudeness. But then her brow furrowed, and her face tightened, like she was in pain.

I really didn't care. I was about to walk away and find another table, but there was a commotion outside the restaurant. A chair fell over, crashing onto the concrete flooring. The other coffee-shop goers had the same look of astonishment as Nan. Some were backing toward the restaurant.

Nan held her hand out and pointed toward the street. And that's when I really heard it.

It was impossible to see, as the sun had set. Although with whatever remnants of sunlight remained and from the occasional flashes of lightning, there was enough illumination to see the clouds and rain, which appeared to be connected to the ground, like an infinity pool of blackness. There was a movement inside the murk, around where the horizon should have been. You couldn't really see it, but you knew it was there; a ghostly shadow of something dark and malevolent. It was as if Hell had spawned the clouds first and then spat out some gigantic Kaiju-like creature that was now lumbering toward us. The Godzilla-like shadow expanded and approached us faster. The noise was almost deafening: a deep roar that caused the earth beneath us to shudder.

I was so taken by this, I hadn't consciously noticed my wife Liz had made a turn onto Main and was only a few yards away from pulling up onto an empty parking spot directly in front of me. The soft streetlight was a beacon for her that she would never reach.

When everyone at the coffee shop saw that the creature was in fact a giant wave of water, it was too late. No time to run, or do anything. That's right when I had my two ignoble thoughts: the one about my being screwed, and the other about my iPhone was going to get ruined.

I still had my coffee cup clutched in my hand when I was flipped end over end, along with the tall table I had been standing up to.

The best I could figure is that the wave first hit the table, then me and then Nan, sending the three of us through the front window of the coffee shop, and somehow the table had to have blocked other debris from killing us.

To this day, I have the flashbacks of that moment when I saw what I thought was my wife's car being carried off by the wave that hit us; inside the car, my wife's terrified face was framed by the windshield.

"Liz!" I yelled.

CHAPTER 4

Nan

Am I alive?

When I woke up, I was submerged, sucking in water, and I was being crushed from above by the man I had just met... Did I just offer myself to him?

My mind replayed what felt like a series of fragmented dreams—more like nightmares—all the while I felt like what life I still possessed was slipping away.

The vivid images from the days before, during and after catching my husband of ten years in the act with another woman. Woman? Hah! She was more like a well-endowed child. I was so shell-shocked and despondent in the days that followed, I couldn't even leave our apartment.

Is this what drowning feels like?

Then there were the images of my best girlfriend Rachel attempting to give me pep-talks each day, telling me that I needed to go out there and take what I wanted from the world.

I can't breathe...

Then last night, Bud called and had the balls to say that he'd like to come back to the apartment, so that he and Chloe could gather his belongings for their little love nest. I hung up and immediately burned all his things in our bedroom fireplace. Who knew all of his sports memorabilia would burn so well? After poking at the burning embers of the only possessions which mattered to him, I had decided to take my girlfriend's advice: go to our neighborhood coffee bar—Rachel suggested a drinking bar, but I didn't drink anymore—and pick up the first good-looking man I could find.

I'm gagging on water that tastes like old coffee grounds.

I first saw Ron from the other side of the outside patio of the coffee bar, after having almost chickened out several times. He was the stereotypical tall, dark and handsome man. His ruddy features spoke of his being outside a lot, and even though he wore a nice dress shirt, I could tell he worked with his hands. They were probably rough and strong. His were the features of a man's man, a breed of man that was all but extinct in this land of metrosexual milquetoasts. He was the one I decided then and there that I'd give myself to.

Complete and utter darkness...

I had leapt from my chair, considering my approach and my words. As I had closed the gap between us, it was obvious he was there for someone else: his eyes darted from his coffee to the street to his phone and back to the street. The whole being-there-for-someone-else thing seemed to motivate me even more. When I saw his wedding ring, I became a bulldog. I knew it was wrong, but I couldn't help it. At that moment, I was filled with both rage and need for revenge; with both sexual yearning and a complete disregard for what harm I did. I wanted to spread my pain to a man, so that he could feel what I felt; but most of all, I wanted to prove to myself that I still meant something, and that I was still pretty in the eyes of another man, even if I wasn't a teenager and I didn't have big boobs.

It wouldn't be long now...

The vivid smells of that moment jolted me: Ron's coffee, his cologne, the embarrassment of his response to my solicitation, "You know, you could have me, if you asked"—I can't believe I said that. He had reeled, like I had sucker-punched him. I felt so horrible and dirty and more embarrassed than I'd ever been. I wanted to die right there. Then God, if there is such a person, seemed to instantly answer my request at that very moment: what sounded like a commercial jet, right at takeoff, roared through the street and into the coffee shop.

A flash of light poked through the darkness—

I don't know how long I was out. But something roughly clutched my shoulders and lifted me out of the water.

That something was Ron.

He held me up like a soaked ragdoll, while I retched out water, coffee and other unmentionables in front of him. And I had never felt such pain as I did at that moment. My chest felt smashed in, as did my right arm.

He yelled something to me from miles away.

When I didn't respond, he hollered, much closer now, "Are you all right, Nanette?"

All right? I thought. My life had ended twice... But then you were there to save me.

I looked up, through a flop of my hair, which blocked most of my vision, but I couldn't do anything about it. I was hacking and I couldn't talk. It felt too painful to even breathe. Yet I held up a thumb to tell him I was okay.

I guess in fact, it was true, I would be okay! I knew it then, even though my body was trying to convince me otherwise.

"I'm so sorry," he said, his voice strong and close now. "I think I sat on you."

"Next time... I get to be on top," I said in a throaty voice I didn't recognize. I couldn't help it. These words just leapt out of me.

He stopped, mouth open. It was obvious he didn't know how to respond to my overt propositions. He slammed his mouth shut. I couldn't see his eyes, but his face sort of reset and then started again. "We were just hit by some giant wave," he told me. "I think the dam broke."

I had no idea what he was talking about, but I didn't care. In spite of every spike of pain with each breath, I felt safe in his presence.

He paused and gave me a once-over, starting with my head and then moving down. It wasn't a sexual regard, but one of concern. I didn't care. I'd take it. Only then could I see a cone of light coming from his hand. Once again, he pointed it directly in my eyes, filling my fuzzy vision with white.

"Can you stand on your own?"

I didn't realize until then that he was still holding me up by the shoulders. Stupidly, I nodded, "Yes!" I really didn't know if I could stand on my own. I didn't want to.

"You look fine," he reasoned and I believed him. "Stay here," he demanded.

Ron looked away from me just then. He turned his cone of light toward the other side of the store and hollered the name Liz. His voice trailed off as he was calling, "Lizzzza!"

Lizzy? I thought. That's the name of my pet lizard. Is she all right? I wondered.

It was Ron's call out to Liz—I was guessing that was his missing wife—that got me worrying about my lizard. My best friend Rachel always chided me about this name choice: "Lizzy? You couldn't come up with a more creative name for a lizard than Lizzy?"

I started to worry about Rachel too. She worked in an insurance office on the ground floor of a one-story, on Main Street, the same street as the coffee shop. She was going to work late today to catch up on some paperwork. "Maybe she left early," I mumbled to myself.

I was still feeling a little dazed by the whole thing, but at least I wasn't hacking up a lung any more. Though my chest still hurt, as did my arm, and I had a horrible taste in my mouth.

Ron, still holding his light, dashed over to the other side of the large room we were in. Only then did it occur to me that we were now inside the coffee bar. The wave or whatever it was knocked us inside. My head spun at that one.

Ron was now helping someone else. His light revealed a soggy but voluptuous woman—that's the type of woman Ron should have and not some flat-chested loser like me. A repressed memory sprang into my head just then: It was Bud's suggestion, not that long ago, that I get a boob job "because"—as he said —"big-chested women get all the perks."

Unconsciously, I grabbed my chest to confirm all of this. The movement of my right arm and the pressure I put on my less-than-ample bosom generated electric shots of pain everywhere. I almost doubled over from it.

A loud crash caught my attention, as a portion of the shop's large window frame collapsed onto a pickup truck partially wedged inside.

I felt an urgent need to get out of that building. While I didn't want to move a muscle, because it hurt too much, I decided to leave right then.

"I'm out of here," I mumbled in Ron's direction, but it hurt too much to project my voice loud enough for him to hear it. Shuffling one wobbly foot in front of the other, I moved toward the front entrance, feeling a wave of panic. The structure surrounding us was just hammered by a tidal wave of water; it could easily fall down, like part of it just did, all while I was busy feeling sorry for myself.

The water was more than waist-high and still moving. But the hardest part was navigating through all the chairs, tables, and other debris floating by, blocking my way, and with almost no light to see where the hell I was going. I stupidly looked up to confirm that the power was out too.

"Dumb shit. Of course, the power's out; it's dark." I still couldn't speak too loud, but the words were coming out easier now.

In front of me was a large table, wedged on its side— it was obvious what it was from its shape. It had lodged itself in between me and the main entrance, as if it was the table's prerogative to keep me here in this coffee shop.

I had had enough. Mustering all of my remaining strength, using my left arm, I yanked at the table, pulling it back and aside. It floated over and out of the way, leaving in its wake a flotilla of debris, including something that was like a large flotsam of suds. I stepped into it, expecting it to part, and was shocked to find it was solid. And soft. I yelped and Ron's cone of light flashed in my direction, illuminating the corpse of a woman; her mouth and eyes were permanently fixed open.

"Oh my God. She's dead!" I screamed and was filled with a wave of nausea.

Blinded by Ron's light and my own panic, I tried to go the other way and run, but the heavy water held my legs down, and my motion and the water's current pulled me sideways, into the body. I banged into one of the dead woman's arms, my face connecting with her puffed-up fingers, and then I went under, while I tried to yell again.

My mouth filled up with more gross water—this time it tasted like death.

Splashing like I was the hysterical twelve-year-old again, after Tommy Johnson told me at the lake that fish like to nibble on girls' toes, I felt utterly ridiculous at my theatrics, both as a child and now as an adult.

Finally, I stood up straight, ignored the pain and got the hell out of there. I practically leapt out the door, which may have been a window, before I made my way out to the street.

It was easier to walk outside, because the water was below my waist now. My head was down, as I was focused on not falling into another next dead body. I looked up when I walked into a overturned Hummer, realizing that I must be in the street. For the second time this week, I was completely rendered dumb with what I witnessed before me.

The air was crackling with sounds: Water raced by, screams and sobs were everywhere, and then, when a momentary splash of light ignited the heavens, I exhaled a giant breath of air I must have been holding onto. This time I didn't feel the pain in my chest. I was just too flabbergasted to notice.

I shot a glance over my shoulder, to try and confirm that I hadn't exited the rear of the coffee shop by accident. I knew I didn't, but I couldn't get my bearings. I looked back and waited only a second for the next lightning bolt.

It was like looking at someone's grown kid, years after you'd seen them last, and they were completely different than you remembered when they were a youth, only yesterday. And you looked for anything that reminded you of the child they once were.

Likewise, looking out on this street I knew so well, my brain tried to find a familiar landmark. Just one. Gone were the recognizable features: Bum Steer, the country-western bar where I had met my scumbag husband, was now an empty space; the Stetson-wearing bull was gone, and so was the rest of the bar.

I blinked several times, as if I expected the vision to change.

The Church of Joshua had exploded outward, as if the wall of water had belted its way through the back and out the front. Its tell-tale crucifix, normally fitted to the facade, was now wedged in between the pet store and the Christian Scientist reading room across the street.

I blinked again, this time finding something familiar.

A block away was Big Ralph's statue. I hated the damned thing, but Big Ralph's BBQ was a staple in these parts, and its gauche Hardee's-like plastic statue of its eponymous owner, with protruding belly—a testament to the results of eating too much BBQ his whole life—was thankfully still there.

But then I glanced to my right, directly across the street from the statue, and when the heavens lit up again, my heart sank.

The two-story Tudor structure that should have risen up above the one-story building in front of me, on top of which sat my apartment, was now half gone.

CHAPTER 5

Ron

"Liz!" I screamed once more.

Enough with trying to save anyone else. I had just helped another woman out of the water, who was shell-shocked and bloody like Nanette, but otherwise not too badly hurt. I had one goal right now: find my wife, while she still had time.

I halted in the waist-deep water and closed my eyes, waiting for the image I had caught only moments earlier to materialize. When I had it, a shudder rippled from deep within my spine and caused every muscle of my extremities to quake. Sure, the water was damned cold, but that was only part of the reason for my shudder. The look on Liz's face was now clearly emblazoned on my brain. Just before she was carried away in her VW, she wore a mask of absolute terror. It was just a flash, and I had to wonder if it was real or imagined. If it was real, I just couldn't reason how she could have survived this. Thinking that this was the last image I'd have of my wife is what made me shiver.

"Oh my Go... Hel..." called a weak voice at the back of the large room.

My eyes flicked open to once again face the watery cemetery inside. It was hard to believe anyone else could be alive. I clicked on my mini-Maglite, thankful I carried it with me today, but wishing I had changed the battery. It flickered once and then cast a weak beam which was eaten up by the dark. As best as I could, I did a quick scan of what was left of the restaurant. I was struck with the devastation. Most of the front was blown out and open. Inside was a waist-high pool with a tangle of floating tables, chairs, debris, and bodies. Outside looked like more of the same.

Partially wedged into the far window was a mangled pickup truck, with its windshield blasted out. Its driver was missing, so it was impossible to tell if it was being driven when the wave hit or was just parked out front.

I thought of Liz and what her car must look like. Where was it?

I could no longer hear, much less see the person who was pleading for help. I had only found two surviving patrons, including the woman I'd helped. Other than me—Nanette had already left—there appeared to be no other survivors inside.

I decided to make my way out of the decimated coffee shop, sloshing one step at a time. I could see the water was still flowing out of the doorways and windows. And the water level had dropped another couple of inches.

Outside, my flashlight gave out completely, so I shoved it into my pocket. I didn't have to wait long for the sky to cast light upon the destruction of our little town. It was one other point of logic telling me that there was little chance that Liz could have survived.

I didn't care, I was going to search for her anyway. Even if there was the slightest chance.

The heavy rain had turned into a light drizzle now. The lightning flashed every few seconds like a red and orange strobe in the sky, revealing a new image of my wet Hell. Screams and sobs surrounded me.

I ignored it all, feeling completely numb to everything. I only cared about finding my wife.

It was so dark, as all the town's power and therefore its lights were out. So I had to wait for each flash of lightning to show me my path through a street clogged with damaged cars, blown over electrical poles, an unlimited hodgepodge of debris, collapsed buildings and floating dead people.

The newest flash lingered, resisted and was then eaten up by blackness again.

I reached out my arms and started to feel my way toward what I remember seeing was a cluster of four or five cars, one of which could have been Liz's silver VW. When I ran into something soft, I stopped.

Another flash of lightning momentarily lit up the area around me and its horror. The soft object was an elderly man, with his face partially caved in. Reacting to the gore, I withdrew and looked past him. An ephemeral image momentarily held of a path around him and the cars, none of which were silver, peppered with white lights. I took a few more steps into the blackness, hands out like bumpers.

Another flash of lightning showed me the way to another couple of cars. So I continued forward, feeling my way in the dark, no longer grossed out by the dead, which I was finding were as plentiful as the upended cars.

When I felt what may have been a dress, or a body part that might have belonged to a woman, I stopped again and waited for the momentary light to confirm it wasn't my wife. I'd then call out her name, in the vain attempt to let her know I was still looking for her, as if she were still conscious and holding on for me to find her.

I don't know how long I was out searching before I heard a familiar but faint voice in the distance. "Ron?"

I froze, holding my breath and focusing all my attention in the direction I thought I had heard that voice, and called out again, this time much louder, "Liz?"

"Ron?" came the same faint reply.

My heart practically beat out of my chest. But I also knew it wasn't my wife.

I walked toward the voice's direction and called out again, no longer a question. "Liz!"

"Ron? Is that you?" It was almost a whisper.

"Nanette?" I asked, as I approached a slight woman, clutching her right arm with her left.

"Oh God, Ron," she breathed and wrapped her unbusted arm around me. "I'm lost. I tried to walk home, but it's destroyed and now I can't see a damn thing. So much death. I came back and couldn't find you. I think my arm is broken because it doesn't work anymore..."

She took several gulps of air, each one ending in a soft "ouch."

"And I think something inside me is broken too. I don't know what to do." She whimpered and shook uncontrollably against me.

I had to admit it. I felt much like Nanette. I was completely spent. I was so tired I just wanted to ball up on a mound of debris and go to sleep. I'd probably die from exposure, but at that moment, I just didn't care. My Liz was missing and most likely dead. Almost everyone else in town was killed from being smashed or drowned.

I knew deep down if I stopped looking for her, and there was even the slightest chance she had survived up until this point, she wouldn't make it through the night. But I also knew I physically couldn't continue: I couldn't see and it was hazardous to move in this stuff while blind; plus I was so exhausted I wasn't thinking clearly and that made me prone to more mistakes; and parts of me were starting to not work, either from fatigue, or trauma, or the cold water, or all of the above.

I absolutely didn't know what to do either. I felt my own whimper inside. Thinking that I probably lost the one person I truly loved made me want to let go, let it out, curl up and let death take away my pain.

But I couldn't give up. It wasn't in my nature.

Liz would want me to survive. But if I continued like this, I probably wouldn't.

Our neighborhood was near the top of the highest hill—perhaps it was untouched by the wave. I'd go home, nap, and come back tomorrow, no later than early morning, to search.

Nanette was still holding onto me, though it almost felt like she was doing this for my benefit and not hers. I could feel her gaze.

"So your home is completely gone?" I asked.

She sniffled. "Yes. But I can't even search to see if any of my stuff made it."

"Do you have anywhere you can go, you know, to stay?"

I felt her shake her head. "No." She started to shudder again. "I have no one... who's alive."

"Come on then. My home is less than a mile from here and it's up on the hill. With any luck it survived. I've got plenty of blankets, first aid supplies and a guest bedroom. You can stay and in the morning you'll help me look for my wife and I'll help you pick through whatever is left of your apartment."

"What will I do after that?"

"I have no idea. Let's take it one day at a time."

CHAPTER 6

Nan

Thump-thump-thump!

I opened my eyes in a panic. It was cave-black. I couldn't see a thing. My hands reflexively shot out to touch something familiar, but only one of my hands made it out of the covers, while the other felt restrained. This accelerated my panic. With my free hand, I found my bundled right arm and squeezed. This sent a jolt of pain throughout my arm and body.

I sat up in the bed, thrust my legs out, and pivoted to where the door should have been. My knees crashed into what felt like a table and caused something unseen to fall over with a deep thud and then a clink. My left hand jutted out to the unseen table, to brace myself from falling over and to act as my eyes in this dark room. To find some sort of firmament.

On top of the table was a cold metal object. My fingers traced the foot-long cylinder—which had a familiar feel—until I found a round rubberized button. I pressed it, and a white cone of light shot sideways across the room.

Thump-thump-thump!

My chest beat like a bongo, but my restricted movements were really pissing me off now. I grabbed the flashlight and flashed it at my arm and chest and felt more puzzled than before I had light. My arm was in a sling and I was wearing men's pajamas. I lifted the giant-sized top and more pieces to this puzzle clicked in place. But I was also more disoriented.

My chest was completely bandaged up, with what seemed like a mile's worth of Ace bandages. I purposely drew in a long breath and instantly felt a spike of pain. But the bandages tightened and kept me from drawing in anything much deeper.

"What the hell?"

My mind wasn't working well either. Everything felt fuzzy.

More panic as I pulled open the elastic of my pajama pants and shot the beam of light down them and saw I not only wasn't wearing any panties, but there was a huge bandage around my thigh.

"How the hell did I get here?" I begged the dark room.

I had to get out. I shone the light around, until finally finding the exit to this nightmare. I ran to it, having to use my hand to pull up the pant cuffs to keep from tripping over them. Opening the door, I looked around, saw a hall and headed down it.

Thump-thump-thump!

The sound was louder now. And as I turned from the hall, I flashed my light forward and caught a glimpse of the front door. I dashed for it. I had to get out.

I fumbled with the lock, my left hand not really working very well. Finally I was able to unlatch it and flung the door open.

Standing in the doorway, blocking my exit, was a very large, elderly man.

"Oh thank God, Li—wait, you're not Liz." He shone his own flashlight into my face, blinding me. "Where's Ronald?" he demanded in a thick Texas drawl.

Ronald, like in Ron? Like in the man who saved you, Nan... After everyone died in town.

It was all a fuzzy jumble, but much of it came back to me at once, hitting me just as hard as the wave of water did. I still didn't remember how my clothes came off and the bandages were put on, but I did remember following Ron to his home. He must have bandaged me up and I must have passed out.

The world started to wobble and I felt so tired.

The old man must have seen the perplexed look on my face and known I was trying to answer his question, since he kindly tilted his light away from my eyes and politely waited for me to collect myself.

"Ahhh..." was all I said, forgetting his question altogether.

"Hi Bob," a strong, but familiar voice boomed from behind me. "This is Nanette."

Bob held out his hand and mumbled something like, "Pleasure." I ignored his hand and watched his expression. He glanced again at me then his facial features dropped as he stared at Ron, who walked around me.

With barely a pause, Ron continued. "Her place got washed away by the wave of water, so I'm letting her stay here. I was about to go back out and look for Liz."

I turned to face Ron. He had a bandage across his head, which was tinted in the middle, I'm guessing from blood. He also had all sorts of scratches on his face and a black eye. He looked like he was in a horrible fight, and lost badly. Otherwise he was clean, dressed in a button-down flannel shirt, pressed jeans, and a rain jacket. He too carried a giant tube-like flashlight like mine.

I wanted to say something before he did. "Thank you for saving my bacon. A promise is a promise. If you can show me, ah, where my..."—I didn't want it any weirder than it felt— "ah, clothes are, I can get dressed and help you find your wife."

"What happened to Liz?" Bob asked, his voice full of emotion.

Ron's eyes welled up and his lashes fluttered, before he answered. "I don't exactly know. I think she was probably swept away in the wave, but I just don't know.

"I needed to bandage Nanette up and catch a nap before going back out..."

"Is there anything Sarah or I could do for you?" Bob asked.

"Yes, look after Nanette. Maybe you could have Sarah check her bandages. She has two deep gashes: one in her belly and one in her left thigh."

I tried to open my mouth in protest, but I didn't know what to say. I was in shock at this revelation and I swear I felt all sorts of pain in the two places he mentioned, but also throughout my body. I also felt in a daze, like I was living in a slow nightmare.

I wanted to go and help Ron find his wife. But I felt so tired. It was like I could go to sleep right there in the doorway and I didn't care what either man said or did. They could just walk around me.

My knees started to give out, and I felt Ron's strong hand grab my free arm.

"Also, I gave her two of my wife's Hydrocodone, because I knew she would be hurting when she woke."

That explains it.

"Absolutely. Sarah will be right over. Anything else?"

"No. Thank you, Bob."

They turned their attention to me.

I felt like I was floating in a dream. Ron and Bob were on each side, walking me back down the hallway that I had just run out of, and then into the bedroom I'd come from. They spun me around and I was seated once again on the bed.

Oh good, I can sleep some more.

"Nanette, stay awake for just a few seconds more," Ron said, his beautiful face in mine. "You're staying here, for now. My neighbor Bob and his wife Sarah, who's a nurse, will look in on you. You're safe right now..."

He was still speaking to me, but my eyelids were too heavy. I let them close.

I heard Ron say something about my ribs being broken, along with my arm. And that there were some old clothes of his wife's in the closet I could wear, that they were going to be donated to a local Christian thrift store.

Before I accepted sleep, without any reservations, I heard Bob saying something about "the world had ended."

CHAPTER 7

Ron

P rior to almost dying for the second time in twenty-four hours, I continued the search for my wife.

The rain had stopped, but the temperature had also dropped another few degrees since last night, and now I wished I had thought to bring my leather work gloves. I blew warmth onto my hands, which were already getting numb. I'm a warm-weather person, which is why I live in Texas. I did not care for this abnormal cold spell.

I'd begin my search on Sycamore and Elm, starting from Liz's office, and then I'd work my way toward the restaurant, walking the path she would have driven. For my own sanity, I had to first confirm that her car wasn't still at her office. Part of me wanted to discount that momentary flash of an image as not reality: It was my own mind making shit up, splicing Liz's face onto someone else's, but it wasn't really my wife. It would be easy enough to confirm. If her car was still at the office, then I would know that I hadn't seen her and there was a chance that she may have survived this thing. I was willing to grasp at any hope, no matter how small it was at this point.

Still, that same image flashed over and over again in my mind: Liz's face tightening, going from confused to panicked as she was being carried off in the wave. It's what kept me from sleeping more than maybe a few minutes before starting up again, even though I was exhausted and needed the sleep.

Scratch that... I'm still exhausted.

In spite of my lack of sleep, just getting dry and warm, made all the difference in the world from last night's search. It also helped to not have to worry about Nanette or anyone else. In truth, I needed to be alone, to face the reality... that I might find her... body.

It was still dark outside, but my best water-proof Maglite carved a conical path of white out of the darkness, a good forty feet in front of me. It was the largest Maglite they sell, and the batteries were brand new. So there was no chance it would crap out before I was done.

Navigating out of my neighborhood was easy. That area was largely untouched by the wave. The moment I stepped into the downtown area, the carnage began. And it was awful.

The water had mostly receded, but in its wake was something similar to what a town looks like after an F5 tornado rips through it, except with water. Each year I'd see the images flashed upon the TV of a Texas town to the North or East of us, getting leveled from a tornado.

Most of the buildings in this area were stick-built and they were the ones which offered no resistance to the wall of water.

The brick and concrete block buildings, as was expected, fared the best. But even these were severely damaged, and some completely destroyed, with whole walls being knocked down or collapsing in their weakened condition.

With each step deeper into town, the minuscule hope I clung to became more distant.

I swear at that time, each side of my mind was vehemently arguing its belief to the other. My hopeful side argued feebly, "She had to have made it because you haven't found a body." My logical side offered an irrefutable rebuttal: "How could she? Just look at this devastation and at all the dead!"

Before this, my hopeful side always lost out to the stark reality of life. My wife was different.

Liz was much more hopeful about everything. She believed in miracles all the time. Her faith in God fueled her beliefs. And so, as impossible as something seemed, she somehow knew that the impossible was possible, even drawing her strength from it.

When a neighbor's child went missing, she told the mother, "Your daughter will return to you." Liz was sure of it, and knocked on doors and hung fliers on every telephone pole in our town. But reality was a cruel bastard. The little girl's body returned home a week later, when Search and Rescue found her at the bottom of a ravine, below her home. My wife was confident of the little girl's safe return up to the last second before reality made hope impossible.

Right now, I wanted to be like Liz, to believe in the unbelievable.

Once again, reality was a cruel bastard.

When I saw her office, I began to weep.

Her building had somehow survived with only minimal damage. My best guess was that the giant mound behind it shunted most of the force of the wave, which had obviously shot right past and down the street, taking with it all of three or four buildings on each side. That was, except her building and most of the one next to it. If she had remained there, she probably would have survived this thing.

If she had only remained there.

I glared at the small parking lot, sandwiched between the mound and the building.

Her parking spot was empty.

My greatest fears were being realized as I knew then that what I thought I saw... that horrific image that replayed in my mind over and over... was in fact real. Liz had left her office—she had even texted me this, telling me she was "leaving now," mere moments before the wave struck. Then she drove to the restaurant, heading down Sycamore, the same street I was now lumbering through. The path of destruction had gone directly down this road: the road Liz had taken before she had turned onto Main and into the coffee shop parking lot. But just as she had made her turn, the wave hit. Her VW had been carried away right then. A half-breath of a moment later, I had seen her when she was most terrified, just before her death.

All of my strength left me, but I lumbered further forward, perpetuated by what I didn't know. I guess I still wanted confirmation.

No, I needed it.

At the intersection of Sycamore and Main, I stopped and lifted my flashlight, even though it felt so heavy, shining my light all around, up one road and down another.

My search had changed so quickly, from saving my wife to now finding her body. And I couldn't deal with it. But I knew I had to.

I hated my damned realistic side.

A part of me wanted to give up. But I still needed closure in my mind, even if I didn't want to accept it. I still needed to find my wife, even though I knew she was gone.

I let my light linger over the coffee shop's facade.

It was pummeled and looked like it might fall over at any moment. Deep pockmarks were chiseled into it, from ground to roof. I examined each mark, trying to imagine if it was a result of Liz's silver VW sub-compact car, its rear windshield emblazoned with Disney World and Jesus Saves bumper stickers.

There was no way to know for sure, so I continued moving forward.

A weak voice squeaked a plea for help, freezing me in my tracks.

I wasn't sure if my mind in its over-taxed state was imagining it. Until I heard it again.

I swung my light onto a cluster of debris plastering the base of a giant oak, which was otherwise stripped of most of its branches and all its leaves. Yet it still stood proud, unwilling to admit it was mortally wounded.

"Helllllpa," the voice called out a little louder.

My heart skipped when I saw it.

In the middle of the cluster was a beat-to-hell silver car, tilted onto its rear, covered in mud and debris.

"Liz?" I yelled and ran to car.

Shining my light on the undercarriage, I tried to find my way up to the driver's side of the car, which was pointed into the air like a rocket ship on a launch pad.

Using the hood of another vehicle wedged into its side, I climbed up and onto the car, carefully steadying myself so that I didn't slide off. I craned my head up, so I could see inside.

Instantly, I knew that it wasn't Liz's VW. But...

The fact that someone lived through the wave in a car just like Liz's gave my hopeful side some fodder to chew on. Was it possible? I wondered.

"Is there someone there?" the female voice asked, hopeful.

I shimmied up the side of the car, to the windshield, which was missing. There, I saw the broken woman inside, belted into the driver's seat. Thrust through the windshield was a pink bicycle, its front fork impaling the woman's shoulder. Shining my light deeper inside, I could see one of her legs was bent upward in an unnatural position. She was covered in her own blood. And I found the windshield, or most of it.

My light snapped upward, finding her face and her glossy eyes that were drilled into me.

"Pretty bad, huh?" she asked.

She was almost severed in two, and frankly I didn't know how she was still alive, hours after this. "Yeah, it's pretty bad," I told her. Didn't seem right to try and convince her of something different, when I didn't believe it either.

"Ron?" she asked.

"Sue?" I said back. I knew she looked familiar. It was Liz's best friend.

She attempted a weak smile. "I'm so glad you made..." Her mouth hung open, her last word dangling, the little curl of her smile locked in.

"Sue?" I yelled at her. I wanted to ask her if she'd seen Liz. They were as thick as thieves and she would have talked to Liz, and maybe even saw her before or after the wave hit. "Sue?" I hollered again. But she was gone.

I huffed out exasperation. And for some unexplainable reason, I started bawling. I didn't care for Sue that much. She was quite needy, and loved money too much. But she was Liz's friend, and so watching her die in front of me was a lot to take in. But it was more than that; it was that little bit of hope that I had so eagerly grasped onto when I first saw the car and heard Sue's voice. And it had slipped away the moment she had died.

I just stared at Sue's stuck expression and cried like I had never done before.

I don't know how much time passed, but when I heard popping sounds in the distance, I looked up.

I flicked off my flashlight, because I could see without it. The sun was out, but whatever light it cast was blunted by wicked-looking clouds blanketing the sky.

Steadying myself on the edges of Sue's car window, I carefully rose to my knees and looked down the valley.

There was a path carved out of my town, into the river, which roared out of sight all the way to Austin.

My wife's car must have been carried down the valley, following the path of the Colorado river and the road that paralleled it. It would be impossible to find her.

I heard voices, followed by the pop of more gunfire.

Off to my left, farther down the road, toward where my shop would have been, were the faint beams of several flashlights.

My stomach turned, as I knew right then who these people were and why they were there. It was Buster's gang of thieves. Like cockroaches that come out at night to feast on leftover crumbs, they were taking what they could from the damaged warehouses and shops. And I could see, by the movement of their flashlights, that they were headed in the direction of my shop. I had to get there first, if I could.

CHAPTER 8

Buster

"You better get moving, or Buster will have your hide," huffed one of Buster's thugs—though I didn't recognize him—to another, who was ransacking Billy's Bait and Tackle.

Buster's men were spread out around the area, going through the stores and warehouses; no doubt looking for the good shit to steal while everyone was trying to figure out what happened and crying for their dead, like me.

Buster wasn't interested in emotional pleasantries; he was only interested in opportunity. And when disaster struck, he knew right away, there'd be opportunity aplenty. It was the way his mind worked.

His men were thugs of various varieties, ranging from the supremely stupid and bumbling to cold-hard killers like Buster himself.

Buster was raised by a father who ran criminal enterprises throughout Texas. Buster lived a good life in a home near mine, overseeing his father's interests in and around Austin. Buster was truly a bad egg, and I'm also quite sure Buster was insane.

Most people stayed away from him, as did I. But those who crossed him generally wound up in the hospital, or worse. And rather than him getting tossed into jail for assault or murder, Buster's father would pay off officials, including our own sheriff, to look the other way. Buster's lone bust was for the rape of a minor, which somehow was knocked down to aggravated assault, but not of a minor. Buster served only a few days before he was out.

It was rumored that the FBI was investigating him to get to his father. And because Buster had used my shop a few times to add modifications to an expensive cigarette boat, twice I had to answer the Feds' questions about him, not that there was anything to say.

I'm guessing nothing stuck, because Buster still roved around town like he owned the place.

And there he was... Buster in the flesh. He strode out of what remained of West Texas Tile and Flooring Warehouse.

Even in the low light, Buster's bald head, prominent Neanderthalic-brow, swollen nose, and dark-set eyes stood out. The orange glow of an ever-present cigarette hung from his lips as he lumbered back toward the tackle shop, while a truck navigated around the debris in the street behind him, awaiting his command.

"Yo, Pecker. You in dere?" he hollered at the tackle shop. He spoke like someone who didn't make it past the third grade, even though he somehow graduated from high school.

A muffled, "Yeah boss. We've got some good shit in here."

Buster took another puff off his cigarette, pulled it out and gave a whistle to the truck lurking behind him. The truck sped up and pulled into the tackle shop's parking lot, just as Pecker came out of the shop with his arms full of long cases.

"Dammit," I whispered under my breath.

I knew Billy Branigan, the owner of the store, pretty well. He sold tackle for fun, but he made his real money selling guns. He was a registered firearms instructor and licensed dealer, selling most of his stuff over the Internet. I had no doubt that Buster's men had found a stash of Billy's firearms he kept locked up.

Buster approached the man, as the truck slowed down in front of them, and said something congratulatory. Then he pointed toward my shop and said, "Fill up the truck. I'm going to check out this warehouse: I want to see if Ronald Ash's boat is still there. If it is, we gonna hook it up to the truck."

All I could think was, That bastard! He had tons of money, and I was always good to him, and he was going to steal my precious boat? I loved my boat, but not enough to die for it.

Still, I knew I needed to get to my shop before he did: there was something there much more important than my boat, especially now.

Keeping low and in the shadows, I quietly made my way closer to my shop on the other side. I had to make my move soon.

When I saw Buster and his men were still focused on what was coming out of the tackle shop, I dashed across the street and into my shop.

It was a wreck, what was left of it.

I knew I didn't have time, but I had to check to see for myself. I ran around the shop to the rear, and almost immediately, I knew the answer.

My precious boat had been parked in the back storage lot, ready for me to pull up with my truck, hitch it up, and drive out to the lake or ocean.

Not only was my boat gone, so was the rest of the yard, and a back portion of my building. All of it was washed away by the water.

It sounds strange to think it, but in a way I was glad. I did not want that rapist son-of-a-bitch Buster getting my boat. I'd even entertained the idea, if I had found it there, of setting it ablaze, just so he couldn't get his hands on it. Each time he had come into my shop for work on his own boat, he'd make me an offer for mine. But I had no interest in selling. It was my baby. I'd made it perfect.

Oh well, I said to myself and then ran around to the side entrance, hoping it wasn't too badly damaged. It wasn't.

The door was broken open, as if it was kicked out from the inside, and I could see the water had been through here too. Inside, everything in my office was ruined.

I heard voices approaching and knew I had maybe one more minute, at the most.

While standing in the doorway, I hesitated, considering my cash register up front. There was maybe a couple hundred dollars' cash inside. I left it and breezed through my destroyed office into the shop and over to a far corner, where I could see what I was looking for.

Among the wet debris blanketing the shop, a black box stood a foot up from the concrete. This strongbox, which was bolted into the floor, was covered in mud, but otherwise looked untouched.

Once there, I fished through my pocket, found the right key and opened the padlock. I yanked off the latch, now not caring if I made noise, and threw open the heavy door. Dry and untouched were some papers, including the deed to my house, the titles to our cars, and two weapons: one AR-15 rifle, never fired by me, and a .357 revolver, which I had fired twice.

Billy Branigan, the owner of Billy's Tackle, and unknown by most of the town, the owner of Billy's Guns LLC, traded me some work on a boat of his for the AR-15. He said it was a top-of-the-line weapon, with optics and everything. I was sure he was getting the raw end of the deal, exchanging what he said was a $3500 gun for about $25 in parts and a little of my elbow grease. But he insisted.

And now I was glad he did.

It never made it home, though, and I never shot the damned thing. My wife hated guns in the house, believing "military-style" weapons should only be in the hands of law enforcement and the military. For her benefit, I kept the rifle and my .357 at the shop.

"You guys check inside. I'm going to the back," Buster's muffled commands echoed through the shop's busted-open front door and windows. I had to leave now.

I slung the rifle over my shoulder and shoved a couple of boxes of ammo into my coat pockets. I quickly checked the .357. It was loaded, and I grabbed one box of its ammo before shutting the door of the strongbox and locking it up.

There was more ammo, but I didn't have any place to put it, and no time.

I glanced at the strongbox again, and shot my light toward the other side of the shop. My boot prints were obvious in the mud and there wasn't any time to cover my tracks. So I turned in the other direction and slid back out the shattered side opening from my office.

Even though it was probably well past ten, it was more like dusk outside, and hard as hell to see through the shadows. And it must have been for Buster's men too, because I could still see the play of light from a couple of their flashlights.

A splash of light tracked toward my direction, but I was already into the next property before any of Buster's gang made it to the shop side of my building to see me.

Without using my flashlight, it was a slow back-track, weaving my way through the thick shadows cast from the piles of destruction which carpeted everything. Speed wasn't most important: I didn't want to be seen.

When I had built a little distance between Buster and his men, I stopped to consider my next move. A thought then hit me and I was thunderstruck.

It didn't even occur to me, until that moment, that what I had left inside the strongbox would put me and everyone else in jeopardy.

Buster's gang would surely find the strongbox and break it open, finding ammo and knowing that as the owner of the strongbox, I had guns now. My footprints showed them that this just happened. But with the missing guns, they'd also find all of our personal documents with Liz's and my names on them and most important, our home address.

I ran the rest of the way home.

CHAPTER 9

Ron

"Is—anyone—home?" I gasped, bursting through the front door of my pitch-black home, out of breath and frantic. In one hand I clutched my .357. With my other, I gave a quick flick of the light switch. As I suspected, the power was still out.

The blackness of the other homes in my neighborhood was noticeable, since the light outside was so weak. And so I had suspected the power might still be out throughout this area: I wasn't expecting it to be back on, just like I didn't expect to find Liz. This is your life, Ronald, I thought to myself. You're a widower now. Your wife is dead and you're worried about a light switch?

"Snap out of it!" I goaded myself. I needed to think logically and remove the emotional ramblings from my conscious mind. And with a serious threat to everyone coming, I didn't have time for emotions. I could process my losses later.

First the power. Our town's power was hydroelectrically generated by the same dam that had most likely had been destroyed, along with the downtown and commercial area. So it was a safe bet that the power wasn't going to be working for a while. Even if the power generation plant was still sending out power, with all of the severed power lines, it would be ages before the power reached us again. We were on our own.

Yanking open the blinds, I doused the living room in a weak light which hardly made it to the dining room.

"Hello?" I yelled again.

Not a peep.

Perhaps Nanette was still sleeping. She was pretty beat up and her body needed some healing.

Scanning the rooms leading to the hallway, I still clutched my .357. I was looking for anything that seemed out of place. And there it was.

On top of the hallway table, leading to my office and the kitchen, was a torn piece of paper, decorated in a foreign and yet very decorative script. Definitely from a woman.

Once in hand, the message was obvious.

Bob & Sarah have kidnapped me.
Hope you were successful.
Thanks for everything!
N.

Bob may have been annoying at times when he found it necessary to show off his intellect. But he was rock-solid dependable. So after reading this, I admittedly breathed a sigh of relief. I took another long breath, shoved the .357 into my pants, trotted back out the door and headed to Bob's.

Our neighborhood was typical of any upscale Texas neighborhood in the Hill Country, a mix of one- to three-story stick-built Tudors, contemporary and ranch-style homes. Most were tasteful, and some were sprawling. About half were full-time residences; the remainder were second homes to the wealthy.

My parents were among the first to build here, constructing their large "dream home" with many rooms for their kids and grandkids, enabling all to be comfortable when visiting. The only problem was that none of their children had kids.

When my parents died tragically on a Regal European cruise, from a mysterious outbreak of some crazy disease, I inherited the house, and my brothers and sisters got most of their money. I still received a sizable enough sum to enable me to be able to buy the warehouse, from which I began my business. Although none of my brothers and sisters were happy, each feeling gypped out of their fair share, I was more than satisfied: I wanted the house because it reminded me of them, and I loved the views of the town below. I didn't care about the money part. Never did.

Bob and Sarah were the second to build in the neighborhood and were close friends of my parents. Maybe even their best friends. When Liz and I moved in, they instantly looked after us, treating us as their own children.

Their house, next door to mine, was one of four in our private cul-de-sac. They and my parents had even joked about connecting the two properties, because they were over at each other's homes so often.

As I approached their driveway, I could hear the low purr of a gasoline engine in back. The soft lights inside told me that they had their emergency generator on.

I tapped on the door and it squeaked open. It was not only unlocked, it wasn't even properly shut, which wasn't at all like Bob.

My hand automatically went to my belt, where the .357 was covered by my shirt tail.

Sarah saw me first and rushed over, her eyes begging the question. When I shook my head she wrapped her arms around me.

The emotions flooded back, but before they turned into tears, Sarah released me and whispered, "I'm so glad you're safe." She grabbed my hand and attempted to lead me to their dining room table a few feet away, where Bob and Nanette were seated, both staring at hot cups of tea and listening to the radio.

I held up when I saw Nanette. She was wearing one of Liz's long-sleeve T-shirts, and around this, a housecoat I didn't recognize. The T-shirt was a gift from me to Liz from a Regal European cruise we had taken with my parents a few years ago. At first, I was a little put out that this stranger was wearing one of my wife's pieces of clothing. But then I remembered it was one of the many clothes we were going to donate to a thrift store run by a woman's shelter in town—probably washed away now like Liz. I had told Bob she could wear anything from that pile.

The next thing I noticed is how beat up Nanette was. Her face was black and blue. The only white, in stark contrast to her purple bruising, were the bandages on her puffy face, which was also carpeted in little cuts.

I felt Sarah's tug, her attempt to bring me in and have me sit with them. But I didn't want to and held my ground.

She then glared at me, reading that it was much more than Liz that weighed upon me. I wasn't yet ready to reveal this.

The broadcast boomed and I focused my attention on this for the moment.

"... volcanic eruptions continue, it may cause further global temperature drops."

A female voice cut in, "We're already seeing a cessation of most air traffic from all the volcanic dust in the air."

The male voice responded. "And cars will soon follow. In fact, most engines and many other mechanical devices will have trouble functioning soon enough, as the volcanic dust works its way into air intakes."

"What about," the female voice cut in once again, "reports we're having of riots and roving gangs..."

I could now feel both Bob's and Nanette's questioning glares.

"What's wrong, Ron?" Bob's voice erupted.

I don't have a good poker face, and so they must have seen right through me.

"I think one of those roving gangs is going to attack us soon."

CHAPTER 10

Nan

The ashfall began the next morning.

At first I thought it was more of the gray snow, but ash is heavier and falls faster. And it's stinky.

Oddly, this was the first and only time I remember discussing it with anyone. And although it was so bizarre to witness, it seems as if we immediately accepted it as part of our new normal. Perhaps if we knew how bad it would really get, we would have at least have discussed it further.

"I wondered when we were going to get this," Sarah said, pulling up beside me at the kitchen sink.

I didn't face her, as I was mesmerized by the work of a lone sparrow, pecking away at the growing layers of ash and ice to get to the water in a birdbath. "You mean the stink, or the falling ash? Or are you talking about the freezing temperatures?"

She didn't answer straight away, and when I glanced at her, I noticed she was staring at something just outside her kitchen window. It was one of those old-fashioned thermometers stuck at just below the 32 degree mark.

"It's been a few years since the temperature dropped below freezing, and that was in winter, not spring," Sarah said, now facing me, but looking down, as if she were having a mental battle about whether or not to reveal her next thought about what was happening outside. She knew what was wrong; she just didn't want to tell me at that moment. Perhaps she didn't want to add to my burden.

After a long moment, her head sprang back up and she drilled her eyes in my direction and said, "Come on, we have a project to work on."

I must have given her a deer-in-the-headlights look, because she then said, "No worries, dear. I'll be gentle on you." She marched over to an orderly little desk area on one of the counters, ripped a few pages off a yellow pad from a small stack of them, and grabbed a pen. Then she shot me a glance that said follow me, and stomped out of the kitchen.

Earlier, I had begged her for something to do when we all woke up. I still felt like hell: Literally there wasn't one place on my body that didn't hurt. But I also felt glad to be alive, and to be looked after by such great people. I wanted to earn my keep while I was convalescing. Not to mention the fact that we were nervous in anticipation of this gang that was coming to get Ron.

It was for that reason that Bob and Sarah insisted that we stay at their home, next door to Ron's; at least until they all felt certain the trouble had passed. When we had this discussion, Ron was reluctant at first. He obviously thought hard about it, but he then glanced at me several times, as if seeking my acceptance, before he finally agreed. It was obvious to me, if I hadn't graced his doorstep, he would have toughed it out on his own. He seems like that kind of guy.

Ron had grabbed a couple of things, including some additional clothes from his wife's 'give-away pile' for me. He had given me an ancient over-sized sleep shirt and a few other things I don't remember. Honestly, I couldn't see changing into anything different than what I had on, because it hurt too much to move, much less change my shirt. So I remained in what Ron dressed me in the previous night and over that, a much-too-large coat of Sarah's.

The men had left a few hours earlier, on a mission to recruit other neighbors to their mutual cause of defending the neighborhood against this gang that was supposed to attack Ron's empty house at any moment. I still didn't see any reason why this gang would make a big deal about a couple of guns Ron had taken from his own locker: This was Texas after all; there were more guns in this state than people. And if they did come to Ron's house, wouldn't they just leave after seeing he was gone?

"Are you coming?" Sarah called from a doorway right off the kitchen, her voice coming from below where it should have been.

I shuffled in her direction and found myself staring down a steep and narrow stairway into a basement. For just a moment, I had a little vertigo and imagined my breaking the remainder of my unbroken bones on the long tumble down the stairwell.

My left hand found the railing and I carefully took one step at a time, following her down. "So what's the project?" I barked, while keeping my eyes glued to the underside of the house's main stairwell, rather than looking straight down.

She didn't answer, but I heard her footsteps in the distance, along with clicks, which added more light below.

When my feet made it to the concrete floor and I let my gaze fall, I couldn't help but stare. I'm sure my mouth was hanging open too.

The room was vast, with much of the floor space covered by wood shelving. Each shelf was packed with full Mason jars and plastic containers.

"What is… all of this?" I asked, bemused.

"Enough food for us to survive whatever's coming," she stated.

"What's coming?" I asked, honestly still unsure what she was getting at.

"Didn't you hear what they said on the radio last night, dear?"

We'd listened to the damned thing for hours, as one reporter after another spoke about how bad it was everywhere: freezing temperatures, streets filled with ash, some cities in shambles, riots, fires, death, and so on.

It wasn't that I didn't believe what they said. I guess it just felt unrelated to our situation even though we suffered our own disaster with the broken dam. But that was local, and we hadn't seen too much of the disastrous effects of the volcanoes. Plus it was just hard to imagine without the visuals. I'm a Fox News and Twitter kind of gal. If it's not on video, it just doesn't feel real. And trying to imagine everything they said was just too much at the time: I was so tired from getting beat to hell, and the stress of seeing dead bodies. But those reports on the radio certainly made an impact with her and Bob.

No, this was set up long before what we were experiencing.

"So did you plan for this?" I asked. It felt like a foolish question, but I didn't see why two people would have so much food, with their kids grown and living far away.

"Lordy, no. Bob and I are what are known as preppers."

"You mean like that funny show, Doomsday Preppers?"

"No. Nothing like that. I've always loved to can the fruits and vegetables we grow, and Bob worried about the other stuff. We just planned to have enough food and water to survive for about half a year, in case something bad happened."

"Yeah, but..." My head was spinning. "How bad could it get? If we're hungry, we just go to the store and get what we need."

I thought of what a food line in Venezuela looked like. Though I never understood how that was possible when that country had so much land and resources. Then I thought of the COVID-19 pandemic, and the panic-buying of TP, water and other supplies. But that cleared up soon enough, and there was always food on the shelves.

I didn't notice right away, but then I heard Sarah was sort of giggling like I had said something funny to her, when I had asked a serious question. I looked at her, my head tilted, plainly not getting the joke.

"Oh my, you're sweet. You don't really know, because I'm assuming you've never been outside of Texas. But do you remember the last bad hurricane that hit Florida? The news showed people going to stores and the shelves were already empty, and that was a few days before the hurricane hit?"

I nodded, because I vaguely remembered that happening last year, where the news played out each day about how bad the pending storm would get, and people had already bought out all the water and plywood from the stores.

"Well, that was only one hurricane interrupting one section of the US. Now imagine all food production and distribution has stopped throughout the US. Remember air traffic has stopped and soon all vehicle traffic will stop. How long do you think the food will last on the shelves if there are no more deliveries?"

I guess my face changed, because she could see I was getting it. I nodded because I could imagine how bad it would be after a few days of no supplies. And Bob and Ron were talking about this thing—whatever this was—lasting months or longer.

"Good. Well that's why we've been slowly building up our supplies. However, with four mouths to feed, I want to make sure we have enough. So you and I are going to do an inventory, and then we'll do some calculations to figure out how much food we really have."

I looked again at the shelves upon shelves of food and couldn't imagine that we'd ever run out of food. Already calculating in my head, I also couldn't imagine Sarah could put all of this on a few pages of paper.

"Don't you think you need more pages?"

Sarah examined the pages in her hand and then nodded. "Yep, you're right. Can you grab two fresh yellow pads from the same place I got these... And a couple more pens and bring them back down?"

"Sure," I said, happy to be contributing, and scurried back up the steps.

I was in the kitchen fairly quick when I heard the doors of a vehicle slam outside the house. I had already completely forgotten about the gang Ron was worrying about, but upon hearing this, my heart started to race. I dashed to a side window that I guessed looked out at Ron's house and peeked through two slats of the horizontal blinds.

In Ron's driveway were two men, who had exited a newer red pickup truck. Both men had military-style rifles and were approaching Ron's front door.

Well, damned if Ron wasn't right after all.

I stared through the two slats in utter disbelief, while I watched them say something to each other and then one ran around the back of the house and the other waited by the front door. He looked like he was speaking to himself and then he balled up a fist and pounded on the door.

Of course it was empty, so no one was going to answer.

A hand touched my shoulder and I shuddered, my heart almost popping out of my throat.

"Sorry to startle you," Sarah said. "What's going... Ah shit, that must be the gang Ronald was talking about."

I must have been hyperventilating, because I found it hard to speak. "Wish... We could... Hear som-ing."

Sarah reached into the blinds, unlocked the window and opened it a crack. An icy wind rushed in and so did a voice. "Come on, Ash. Our boss just wants to ask you a few questions."

Sarah knelt down beside me and with her hands, parted the blinds further so that we both could easily see through them.

To our shock, the front door opened, but it wasn't Ron. The gang member's partner—the one who ran to the back—came out of the front door shaking his head.

We knelt there for what must have been a while, because they made several trips in and out of Ron's house, each time with boxes of Ron's stuff.

At one point, Sarah had had enough of their thievery and was going to show them what she said was the 'business end of her shotgun,' but I insisted that her shotgun against their military-style rifles was not going to end well for us. We just needed to be quiet and watch.

At some point, they decided they had stolen enough and made their way back to the truck cab. The one who had pounded on the door took up the driver's seat and the other went to the passenger side.

We heard a muffled but clear enough voice from the driver. "Are you sure you didn't see a boat anywhere? Buster really had a hard-on for that boat."

The other man shook his head and stood up high on the step-up of the Ram and looked out around the neighborhood and said, "Maybe Ash parked it in a neighbor's yard."

His gaze fell upon us and our open window and he stopped.

At that moment, I knew in my gut they had seen us.

Sarah let go of the blinds. And just before she slammed the window shut, I heard, "Did you see that? Two women watching us next door. Come on, let's get 'em."

CHAPTER 11

Ron

Almost all of the houses were soulless.

"Remind me of the purpose of this? Most of these places are empty because their occupants are either living someplace else or they've died from the wave. And those who are home are either not in any physical condition to defend this neighborhood, or they won't believe there's anything more serious going on than one local disaster, which has come and gone."

My words sounded hollow through the N95 mask. I squinted through my goggles at Bob, waiting for a reply as our footfalls squeaked in the gathering ashfall.

"They'll believe in a few weeks, won't they?" he chuckled through a black gas mask, which made him look somewhat malevolent. Every time he spoke in the thing, I had images of Darth Vader dance through my head.

"Would you be serious for one minute, Bob?" I said, tiring of his condescending tone. We didn't have time for this. Buster's men could show up at any time, and meanwhile Bob kept us busy with useless activities like doing welfare checks on our neighbors. None of these people—the few who were home—would take up arms to protect the neighborhood: Most were older rich people who were too self-indulgent to go outside of their properties, much less put themselves into a risky situation. Besides, it wasn't the neighborhood's problem, it was mine.

I'd only then realized that Bob had halted and was glaring at me, hands on hips.

When he had my attention he stated, "I am taking you seriously, Ronald. But all of you don't get it. You never have. Everything we consume in our lives: water, food, medicine, heat, banking, commerce, information... Everything is dependent upon all of the parts of the machinery of our society constantly spinning. You take one cog out of that machinery—just one—and the whole thing stops. And when it stops, society breaks down.

"It happened with Katrina: Mobs took over the flooded streets and stole, raped and murdered without any fear of repercussions. And that was just one storm.

"We came close with COVID-19, but the Internet infrastructure continued to hum along. And grocery stores were considered 'essential businesses,' and so were the supply trucks which kept bringing in fresh supplies so stores could constantly stock their shelves. People never felt the pain of doing without their next meal or streaming their next movie.

"This will be different.

"Imagine what will happen after a couple of weeks, when everyone in this country is out of food, and they've been without their precious Internet and TV fixes, and they've been freezing in their homes, because they have no heat. Many will become victims, simply curling up and accepting death. But the rest will become desperate. And desperate people do desperate things."

I had not heard Bob say so much, uninterrupted, since I had known him. I wished he'd address the point of my comment, but he obviously had a speech he wanted to deliver.

"But those desperate survivors are not the ones I'm worried about. There will be the gangs, like Buster's clan, who know there will be no accountability; those who have no moral centering and believe the world and its people are put there for them to take and do whatever they want. They are the ones I worry about." Finally he took a breath.

"Okay-okay," I told him. "I understand all of that. And believe it or not, I don't disagree with you. I'm just wondering why we're spending the time door knocking, when most of these people are probably part of the curl-up-and-die variety. Certainly none of the folks we've spoken to today, except maybe one, would take up arms against thugs like Buster's men. So why isn't this a complete waste of our time?"

"Good God, Ronald, you can be daft at times, you know that? You missed the whole reason for our exercise today. I wasn't trying to find able-bodied neighbors to lead some resistance against Buster's band of idiots. I wa—"

Pop.

We both caught our breaths and spun around to where we heard the shot.

The world around us was a silent landscape of cascading gray.

Bob lifted an arm and pointed to the next block. And I knew it too.

He was pointing at our block.

Where we had stopped, and I had been on the receiving end of Bob's lecture on American lethargy, was at an intersection of one road and our little street, which dead-ends at a cul-de-sac. At that cul-de-sac were Bob's and my homes. From where we stood, we couldn't see Bob's house, but we could see most of mine: Backed into my driveway was a red pickup truck. The same truck I witnessed last night used by Buster and his men to steal goods out of stores and warehouses like mine.

"It's them!" I yelled, yanked the revolver out of my pants, and started running.

Bob hollered from behind, "I'll check... on the women. Be careful... These men... killers."

I couldn't remember the last time I'd run that fast before, and certainly not with a mask on.

Before I knew it, I was in front of their red truck, with my .357 aimed right at it. Both doors were wide open, but no one was inside or out.

Boot prints in the ash circled the truck and led to and around the house.

My front door was also wide open.

I slid past the truck, glancing quickly into the bed, and saw boxes of my own stuff haphazardly piled inside. The little bastards broke in and were stealing from me right now, I thought. The shot must have been them thinking they'd found me hiding or something.

My thumb found the revolver's hammer and pulled it back, just as I stepped over the threshold.

Boot prints of gray ash were everywhere inside.

Bob's hefty foot falls sounded behind me, but I kept my focus on what was in front of me. I guessed Bob was just about at his front door by now.

I slipped my mask down to my neck and tried to repress my own rapid breathing so I could listen for the sounds of my robbers. Nothing.

My study was where I kept some of my most valuable possessions, so I headed that way. At the turn to the kitchen, I stopped to see my back door stood open, shards of glass around it. "So that's how they got in," I whispered to myself.

Pop-pop-pop.

Boom-boom.

Pop.

I ducked at the first shots; hearing them from behind me, I thought the bastards got the drop on me somehow. But the second shots were from a twelve-gauge shotgun... Bob's shotgun, which he had left with Sarah, to protect her and Nanette.

Realizing this, I spun around and dashed back out my door.

Instantly I saw the signs.

Signs that I should have seen when I had first run to my house: the footprints leading from the truck to the open side window of Bob and Sarah's house, the tattered blinds hanging out of it, as if the house had puked out something nasty it had been forced to swallow.

The men had broken in this way.

I rushed through Bob's front door, left ajar, holding my .357 in front of me. My finger was ready to dispatch these men. This time I didn't try and worry about making any noise by holding back breath, letting my chest heave normally.

A voice.

From the kitchen I heard, "Put pressure here," followed by the thumps of rapid steps, followed by a door being thrown open.

Sounds of crying. Nanette's.

I dashed toward the kitchen and seized up just before entering.

Two men lay motionless on the floor, growing pools of blood beneath each of them.

Then I saw Nanette through the kitchen entry.

"Nanette, are you all right?" I huffed.

She slowly turned her head up to me, just as I was standing over her...

And Bob.

"They... shot... him," she said in between sobbing heaves. Her one good arm pushed down on a bunched-up shirt over his belly. Blood everywhere. His blood.

Bob's complexion was as pale as Texas mud in summer. His chest was barely moving. His eyes drilled into me. His lips hardly moved, but I heard him saying, "Ronal..."

He was calling to me.

I leaned over him while his lips moved again, and he spoke in a dull whisper. My ear pressed almost against his lips so I could hear him.

One of his mitts grabbed mine and squeezed like a small child.

Right then, I knew he wasn't going to make it. I was about to hear his final words.

"Tell Sarah I'll always luv hur... Promise me, you'll keep hur saf..."

"Yes, of course I will," I whispered right back.

"... And don't wai... Get bodies ou... Goto empty houses and git supplies... Prepare fo wors... Ice a"—his voice was almost imperceptible now—"Git books on garden... Greenhousss... And if need escape, use secret paaa..."

I waited and listened, hoping he'd finish his final thought, or add to it. But he said nothing more.

I looked back at his face.

Peaceful. Silent.

He's gone.

"Nooo!" shrieked Sarah from behind. She dropped an armful of dressings she had collected up for her husband and fell on top of him, sobbing.

Nanette sat down from her kneeling position on the floor and wrapped her one good arm around her chest, her sleeve saturated in blood up to the elbow. Convulsions of anguish took over.

Worse than feeling utterly helpless, I had just committed to looking after Sarah from now on, along with Nanette.

I stood up and just watched these two women bawl, while my mind attempted to decipher Bob's last words.

Overwhelming sadness and gloom swept over me and I turned away, so that neither of them would see what I felt.

Just then, the kitchen lights flickered and went out.

CHAPTER 12

Nan

I could almost ignore the blood and the piss, if I let my mind wander.

Sarah had us doing busy work once again. It was physically taxing and truly disgusting. But while we cleaned up the gore from the floors, I thought about what had happened.

It was mostly a blur.

When we saw the one man look our way, we had run.

I realized we'd forgotten to close the window. But that was a good thing, because right after we left the room, one of the two men shot at us, shattering the window and the frame in our absence.

I wonder now if Sarah had left the window open on purpose. The shot fired her up further, and she wanted to fight these men. I wanted to hide. I was so terrified.

She led us to the basement entrance, off the kitchen, where she said we could surprise them, and if necessary we could always lock ourselves inside the wine cellar. "But first, if either man comes into the kitchen, I'll blast them."

In anticipation of this eventuality, we waited on the stairwell, me shivering and Sarah pointing Bob's double-barreled shotgun at the closed door. If someone so much as touched the handle, she'd let them have it.

Right then, we heard the men breaking through the living room window, followed by their heavy footsteps on the first floor.

When they were in the kitchen, I held my breath. Sarah's finger hovered near the trigger, then it moved onto the trigger. It was about to get noisy, and I turned my head away, plunged a finger into my closest ear and held my breath.

That's when something happened that neither of us expected.

We heard the front door fly open with a crash, followed by a familiar voice calling, "Sarah?"

"Oh no, it's Bob," I whispered.

Sarah was already out the basement door, turning the corner, out of sight when the gunfire erupted.

Bob must have gotten it first: three shots. Then Sarah took out one. And then Bob got the other one. It was over when I came out from hiding.

After that, I'm not sure. We had both been on the floor crying away forever, when I noticed Ron say something to Sarah, who nodded and stepped away from Bob.

Sarah helped Ron wrap up Bob's body in a sleeping bag, zipping it up, and then they dragged him into the garage. Sarah said the cold temperatures in the uninsulated garage would preserve him until they could bury him.

Then Ron rolled up the dead men in two throw rugs and dragged each outside, tossing both into the bed of the red truck they had driven up in.

He gave Sarah a hug and told me his plan was to get rid of the bodies and the truck so that there was no connection between the dead men and Ron's home. Then Ron left us again, to deal with each other and the thundering silence of our sorrows.

Sarah had a different plan. She pulled out buckets, filled them with water from their well, and handed me one, along with a left-handed glove and a sponge.

I had not been around dead bodies before. But it now seemed to be a regular thing. I honestly don't know how I did it; guess I figured if she could do it, so could I. Somehow, I ignored the smell and mechanically went about cleaning up the area where both men had died. Sarah dumped my soiled water and brought us both fresh pails.

Scrubbing with one hand was difficult and painful. But the exercise kept me from focusing on my own sadness.

Sarah didn't say a word the whole time.

When we were done, only our broken emotions and haunting mental images of the incident remained: There was absolutely no physical evidence that someone had died there.

Then Sarah had us board up the broken window.

Through all of this, I was frankly blown away by Sarah's resilience. She'd watched her husband of forty-some-years die, and she just went on with life. Because she had to. I never saw her cry after he'd died. Not once.

After all of this, we went throughout the house, checking all the windows and doors, to make sure the entire place was secure.

Finally, she donned a gas mask to protect herself from the ash—which was falling even heavier then—and went out back to fill up the empty generator, fired it up and flipped a switch, sending rolling shutters down on all of the windows.

The entire house fell into a protected darkness.

After turning off the generator, to conserve fuel, I followed her to the basement, her flashlight leading the way. Sarah snatched an oil lamp from one of the shelves, lit it and set it on a table, surrounded by two chairs. She told me she could have used the light, which ran on a car battery and was recharged by the generator, but she wanted to conserve the fuel now. We would conserve everything from now on.

I sat at a table in the middle of the vast storage room, surrounded by floor-to ceiling shelving, and waited for her to stop.

She stepped up to one of the shelves filled with wine bottles, glared at one particular shelf for a long breath and then sighed loud enough for me to hear. She carefully slipped out a bottle of wine, snatched another object, and two bulbous wine-glasses. All of these she set on our table. Then, like a wine sommelier, she used the strange object, which was an ostentatious bottle-opener, to pop open the cork, fill both glasses, and finally poured herself into the chair opposite me.

"Every year," she said to the glass, "we've had a California vineyard make bottles of wine for us, based on our request. They'd take care of everything, even slapping our own silly personalized label on each bottle, and then they'd ship four cases of that year's personalized wine to us. This is from a special case of Merlot they bottled in commemoration of our fortieth wedding anniversary. Each year we'd open a bottle of this on our anniversary day, and drink in celebration…"

She paused to take a sip and swallow. She sniffled and a small convulsion, like a shiver, rippled in her chest.

"We"—she sniffled twice—"were going to open this tomorrow." She wiped away a couple of tears, before they could sneak out much further, and then she drank down the entire glass of wine in one fluid gulp.

I glanced at the bottle, while she inhaled her wine, and noticed the label. Fortieth Anniversary. And below it, a silhouette of two people holding hands, with a sun rising behind them, and the words Perfect Pair.

I couldn't help it. My own tears had been welling up during her short story. They burst out and streamed down my face. They were the 'perfect pair' and now he was gone. Forever.

I must have been so focused on my full wine glass, and paying no attention to Sarah, that she startled me with her voice. "What did my husband say… before he died?"

"What?" I asked, not understanding the question.

Her eyes drilled holes into mine. "What did Bob say to Ronald before he died?" She articulated this very clearly, without the smallest hint of emotion.

"Ah, I'm sorry, Sarah, but I didn't hear what he said." This was true. But there was more to this and she knew it. I knew, because Ron had told me, and he would tell

Sarah after he disposed of the bodies. "Ron said that Bob told him that he loved you and he made Ron promise to look after you."

"Yes, I know all that. Ronald told me this too, when I insisted. But what else?"

"Ah, that's all I know, at least that's all that Ron told me. Why?"

"When had I returned with the bandages, I could see Bob speak to Ron for a lot longer than would be necessary to tell him what you just repeated. I know my husband; he would have given Ronald some sort of specific instructions on how to protect all of us— specific things he would have wanted Ronald to do."

"Maybe it was about disposing of the bodies?" I guessed. But I looked past Sarah and thought about it. She was right; Bob's lips were moving a lot longer than what was needed to tell Ron what he revealed to me. Perhaps it was a more personal message, one that Ron chose not to tell Sarah until later. If it was, it was something that he didn't want to worry Sarah about.

"Perhaps you're right," she said. "I just wish—"

Thump-thump-thump.

It was a rapid knock from upstairs, the front door.

I practically shot out of my seat and bumped into the table, sending their anniversary bottle of wine sideways.

Sarah's hand caught it in time. Then she calmly rose, sashayed over to another table to grab her shotgun, opened the breach to make sure it was loaded, snapped it back, and marched up the stairs, pulling back each hammer like this was her normal process of answering the front door.

"You might want to stay down here, in case it's someone else who's not friendly," she said, completely devoid of any emotion.

There was no way I was staying down there by myself. Even though I was terrified of who that might be, I was better off knowing. "Nah, I'm right behind you," I said. I hesitated and grabbed Ron's cannon—the one he had left with me for our protection—grunting a little at the weight, and trotted up the steps behind her, tripping once and almost falling.

Thump-thump-thump sounded again from the door, followed by a muffled holler. "Help!" It was a woman's voice.

Sarah said nothing. She strode to the front door, lifted her head to the eyepiece, and only then did her whole demeanor change. It was like she had transformed back into the person I had first met: the kind caregiver.

She laid the shotgun up against the wall, behind the door, out of sight, and threw open the door.

Cough-cough! "Oh thank God," bellowed a woman standing just outside. "It's my husband, Sarah. He's badly—cough-cough—hurt." The woman shot a glance past Sarah to me and then back to Sarah.

"Where is he?" Sarah asked.

"Back home. He's bleeding badly."

"We'll meet you there. Go!" Sarah commanded, then turned from the door and ran past me. "Come with me," Sarah barked. "We're going to get my supplies and check on Phyllis' husband. I'm not letting someone else die if I can help it."

CHAPTER 13

Ron

B ob's final words were clear: "Don't wait. Get bodies out. Go to empty houses and get supplies. Don't wait! Prepare for the worst... Ice age."

I let those particular words ramble through my head as I navigated through our town with the headlights off.

It was the middle of the day, and yet with the thick cloud cover and falling ash, it was more like dusk. But I didn't want to risk being seen with two dead men in the bed of what could have been a stolen pickup truck.

Bob's words were part warning and part pleading. He knew something bad was coming, and apparently he'd been preparing for it for some time, both he and Sarah. And although Sarah struck me as someone made of sterner stuff, I opted to not tell her all of what Bob said. It just seemed like too much of a burden to lay on someone all at once: First you lose your spouse of forty-plus years, and then you find out the world as we know it is actually ending... All on the same day?

I shook my head just thinking about this.

And then my thoughts quickly returned to Liz.

I have to admit to you, that with every moment I was alone, like this one, my heart felt ripped out of my chest and I was transported back to two nights ago when I saw her carried away from me, forever. I still couldn't accept it.

I shook my head more violently this time, like an Etch-a-Sketch, erasing my mental screen and readying it for my next mental scribbling. This was constant.

I resolved two things right then.

As brutal and as sudden as Bob's death was for Sarah, seeing him dead may have been a blessing for her, versus Bob just not coming home one day... like Liz. At least Sarah knew he was gone and she could ultimately make peace with that. I would never have that resolution... Or that peace.

The next thing I resolved was to follow Bob's final requests. To the T.

"Don't wait for anything! Prepare for the worst, which is the coming ice age." I proclaimed this to the windshield, paraphrasing Bob's words as I understood them.

He seemed to think that this was the start of it: a new ice age. That was the worst-case scenario. And I guess I believed him, without any second-guessing. So I would do as he asked: I would do what was necessary for Sarah, and Nanette, and yes, even Liz, though she wasn't ever coming back.

I gunned the truck's engine around a curve in the road. The back tires fish-tailed a little on the thickening layer of ash that seemed to cover everything now, before grabbing the road again.

A new sketch came to mind, one that I quickly erased.

It would be a shame to get rid of this truck, because it was a solid vehicle. And knowing what was coming, I was sure we would need more vehicles. But keeping this one was the kiss of death for us. If we were lucky, Buster's men wouldn't connect us with this pickup and the men who had driven it to my house. From what the women said, they had come to steal my boat, which may or may not have been on Buster's orders. No, the truck had to go, along with its drivers.

Nanette had convinced me that whatever meager guns and ammo I had, in a state where everyone had at least one gun, would otherwise not merit another thought to Buster or his men. I even started to suspect that we might be able to avoid Buster altogether, and that he probably wouldn't bother us as well, at least for a while: There were so many other supplies out there than what we had. And even those were unknown by anyone. At least that was the hope and it would have to do for now.

I slowed the truck way down—I wanted to avoid sliding on the ash and crashing—and made my final turn, immediately catching a brief glimpse of the building I was looking for. I had only been there once. With Liz. My wife had taken care of our household finances, including setting up our insurance, and she did this through her dead friend Sue Ellen Simpson.

The sign on the corner unit of the commercial building said Sue Ellen's Property & Casualty. And at that moment, the image of Sue's bloody face and mangled body, just before she died, slammed into my head. I shook it away, along with perpetually reoccurring images of my wife, as if the two were interconnected. I adjusted my painter's mask and goggles and then exited the truck into a soupy muck of gray glop, in front of the one-story building entrance.

A quick glance confirmed what I had hoped: there was no one else around.

This place was just outside of the downtown zone that was destroyed by the wave. My reasoning was that it was one of many professional buildings on the main road and wouldn't likely be visited by its worker-occupants. If they had survived, they would be more focused on their own homes and families. Plus I knew Sue Ellen wouldn't be coming back again. Finally, it seemed like a safe enough place to stage my subterfuge, so when Buster's men found these two, there would be no one else around to suffer his wrath.

I stiffened up and kicked in the door, knowing its weak point. It was all part of the plan to make it look like these men had broken in. Then I hauled each bundled-up dead man inside over a shoulder, taking care to not let any of their blood drop, except where I wanted.

Forensics was not the concern here: Two dead thieves would not be given much regard in a world of so many dead. And if Bob was right about his apocalyptic estimates, they might be disregarded by the outside world altogether. I just wanted to make sure these two were easily found by Buster or his men, if and when they went looking for them.

Each man was carefully unfurled from his rug cocoon. Then each was held up, as if standing. Then each was released, letting gravity do its job. The goal was to make it appear like they were hit by gunfire and then fell over where they stood.

In their laid-out positions, I maneuvered each of their heads for their respective 'kill-shots,' to make it appear as if each doomed thief gave their killer a glance before finally buying it. Maybe I watched too many movies or read too many books. But this whole way of thinking seemed logical to me.

Then came the hard part.

I unslung my AR-15, the one Billy had traded me for work. I still hadn't shot the damned thing. Even Bob had used it, killing one guy; Sarah got the other with a shotgun blast. I knew that I needed to fire this thing and get somewhat familiar with it, and I was pretty sure I needed to do this fairly soon.

I understood the basics: It was a mechanical device, like any other, and I knew how things worked. I just needed to get somewhat proficient with it, and quickly.

I held the rifle in my hands, but was reluctant to go any further. The thought of what came next tore at my gut. My first target practice was going to be far more difficult than I realized.

"Good God, Ronald. Don't be such a damned wimp!" I chided myself. If I couldn't shoot an already dead person, how in the hell am I going to be able shoot at a live one?

I took aim at the first man's head, held my breath and pulled the trigger.

Nothing.

"Shit."

I forgot. Turning the weapon sideways, I saw the problem and clicked the safety to FIRE.

Much quicker than the first time, I raised the weapon, took aim and fired.

Boom!

My ears rang like church bells on Sunday.

In the confines of the small waiting area of Sue Ellen's insurance office, the rifle was far louder than I could have imagined.

I looked up at my first target, a bulbous man in his thirties who returned my gaze: His was vacant. A thin smile curled up his bearded mug, punctuated by a giant black mole on his nose. But there was not a single mark from my rifle, even though I was aiming right for his head.

"How in the hell could you miss him? You're only ten feet away," I yelled at myself.

I took one step closer, brought the gun up, took a breath and fired.

Direct hit.

The fat man's head jerked, and blood—black as crude oil—leaked out of the new hole I had punched near the edge of his forehead. My stomach lurched right then.

Breathing out, I took in the next one.

He was an emaciated man, much younger than the first, with thin, long blond hair. This kid should have been a surfer, hanging out on a beach, whispering sweet lies to girls in bikinis. He should not have been one of Buster's thugs.

The kid's head was tilted up against a chair leg, as if he were looking right at me. His face was locked in painful terror, as I would have imagined, being on the receiving end of a twelve-gauge shotgun blast.

I sighted in the kid's eye, rather than forehead: I wanted to shoot only once more and be done with this exercise. The kid's eye danced in my gun sight, as if he were moving.

Of course, he wasn't.

Boom.

Either my hearing was dying or I was getting used to the noise. I looked up and saw that I'd only nicked him.

"Dammit!"

I took one more step toward him, aimed once more at his eye and without hesitation, pulled the trigger.

This time I didn't miss.

The kid's head jerked, but not much: I had gotten him right in the eye socket; his eye was gone now, and what exited was a grotesque spray of brain matter and blood. The spatter of surfer-dude's organic material coated the chair, the carpet and the back wall. A bloody chunk slid down the wall.

I bent over and puked.

Well, that didn't go according to plan, did it, Ronald?

My heart thumped so hard, if I could hear any more, I was sure I would have heard my ribs crack with each beat.

Apparently I wasn't very good at shooting dead people. But I did what I came to do: dispose of the bodies, set them up to be found, and I now knew how to use my weapon. I spat out a mouthful of bile and prayed to God that I wouldn't ever have to do this again.

The final part of my elaborate plan was to get rid of the two rugs. But now I just wanted out. I rolled up both rugs together as one and hoisted them onto my shoulder. I figured I'd toss them over a fence a block or two away.

After a quick check of the premises, feeling satisfied, other than the puke part, I headed to the front door.

I sucked in my breath and came to a dead stop.

Outside the partially-open door, where I parked the red pickup truck, were two men. They were inspecting the truck. Talking. One looked in my direction. Then he pointed right at me.

"Ah, shit," I mumbled, dropped the double-rug and dashed to the back of the office.

CHAPTER 14

Nan

"Stand back, I need room," Sarah demanded from each of us.

I pulled Phyllis back from hovering over her unconscious husband, whose name escaped me.

When we had arrived, he was mumbling about trying to save a woman and that he hurt.

While Sarah tried to set a compound fracture in the man's arm, he woke up thrashing. Both Phyllis and I rushed over to hold him down, while Sarah prepared a needle and a vial of some medication I couldn't see.

The man resisted at first and then gave up. He looked at his wife and said, in tears, "I couldn't save her. I couldn't save Li..."

Sarah had given him an injection and he was out again before he could finish his statement.

"I've got him now. Could you please get me something to drink, while I finish up?"

I suspected that was Sarah's way of getting Phyllis away from him while Sarah worked some more on the man. I gave Sarah a look and she nodded for me to go too.

When I first saw Phyllis at the door, she struck me as older than Sarah, by a dozen or so years. Now, as she prepared tea on a propane cook-top, she appeared to have aged even more.

About the time the tea was ready, Sarah had come into the kitchen, and Phyllis' head snapped in her direction. "It's okay." Sarah held a palm up. "He's resting now."

Sarah laid her doctor's bag on the kitchen counter and took up residence on a stool beside me. "He's lost a lot of blood, and he had several broken bones, including his arm, as you saw. But I'm sure he's fine. I put another blanket over him. But you'll want to..." She stopped to accept the tea, and drank the hot liquid with a satisfying moan.

"... but you'll want to keep an eye on him. Let him sleep, but keep him warm."

I listened and sipped on my tea. I wasn't a big tea fan, but this was the best stuff I'd ever tasted. It was exactly what the doctor ordered. But I was curious about what happened and if Phyllis had heard something about what was going on outside of this neighborhood.

"Do you know what happened to him?" I asked.

Phyllis set her cup on the counter in front of us. She looked up in the air and told us her husband's story.

"I found him at our front door, just a little while ago, after hearing some scratching at the door. I was beside myself with worry over Ethan. He hadn't come home the night before last, and I couldn't reach him on his phone—I couldn't reach anyone on my phone—and I didn't want to go looking for him and have him come home and me not be here.

"So I find him at the front door and I think he's dead, but then he wakes and thrashes"—she looked up at Sarah—"just like he did now. Anyway, he saw me and said, 'Thank God you're here' and walked with me to the living room couch where you found him. I could see right away he was badly hurt, but I didn't see the bone sticking out until later; he was hiding that from me.

"He told me he'd just left from work when the wave hit. He'd been walking to his car when he heard the booming wave, and so he ran, but it caught him and sent him several blocks away before he found himself dangling from a tree, right beside the roaring river. When the water receded a little, he said he climbed out and found dead bodies piled up around the trees lined along the river. But he also found someone alive, at least at first.

"He told me the woman he tried to help was Liz Ash —"

I snapped my head in Sarah's direction, and she in mine at the same time. I grabbed her arm and squeezed like a vise. We drilled our eyes back at Phyllis and held our collective breaths.

Phyllis watched us and continued, "Yeah, Ronald's wife. Ethan said that she was hanging outside of the windshield of her VW, which was propped in the tree beside where Ethan had been. Ethan tried to get to her and could see she was in bad shape. Barely alive. And I guess when he put his weight on the car, it gave way. It came crashing down, throwing him from it, and then it splashed into the river."

I guess my grip on Sarah grew several points tighter, because she pulled at my hand and then ripped it away.

I saw Sarah's eyes fill up again. I think I might have started to cry too, even though I didn't know Liz, and earlier was hitting on her husband. But I knew Ron and I knew Sarah, and I knew how much they cared about Liz.

Phyllis continued, "I guess Ethan broke his arm badly when he fell from Liz's car... He said there was nothing else he could do to save her, Sarah."

Phyllis' eyes welled up too. "Please tell Bob and of course Ronald I'm so sor—"

Sarah shot out from her chair, its legs screeching against the tile. She snatched the leather doctor's bag from the counter. "I have to get back. Come on, Nanette."

Phyllis didn't know about Bob. How could she? It just happened, and we'd been so busy with Ethan...

Phyllis added further to Sarah's discomfort before she could escape, bear-hugging her arms to her side. "Thank you so much for coming. Please tell Bob—"

Sarah ripped free, snatched up her gas mask with the white S on it, and bolted for the door. I trailed not far behind.

"Is everything all right?" Phyllis begged, unsure what to do, trudging behind us.

At the door I turned and shook my head no. I wanted to tell this woman, but it wasn't my place. I was a guest in their community, caught up in the middle of all this heartache. And now, to find out Ron's wife was in fact dead... My heart broke for him, and for Sarah.

I started to sob, and ran out the door after Sarah, leaving Phyllis perplexed in the doorway.

I found Sarah halfway between the two houses, back to me, her head slung forward, face obscured by her gas mask, shoulders down, convulsing. I came around to her and wrapped my one good arm around her, the only thing I could think to do. I held her, trying to offer my comfort, and softly whispered, "I'm so sorry, Sarah." My voice sounded foreign through the painter's mask I wore.

From our embrace, I watched the gray ash continue to trickle down to the ground. It was quiet, like a shroud of death that was covering all of us.

At some point Sarah breathed out a sigh. "Ethan won't make it through the night."

"What do you mean?" I asked. I didn't think someone could die from a compound fracture.

"He has internal bleeding. There was nothing I could do for him. I just didn't want to be there when he died. I couldn't do it aga—"

Sarah stopped mid-sentence, shuddering—I thought it was her crying, but it wasn't.

The shuddering grew stronger and the world around us groaned.

We both fell over and I realized, it's another earthquake.

CHAPTER 15

Ron

I'm trapped!

Desperate to leave, I had turned in the wrong direction. I did a quick double-back to the only other door which must have led to a back exit. But I was too late.

"Yo look"—cough-cough—"there they are," said a Sumo-wrestler-sized man who waddled inside, and then stopped at the two rugs I had dumped in haste. He coughed some more, turned his back to me, hacked up and spat a gray-black wad of phlegm, and pointed at the two dead men.

"Dammit," I whispered, while ducking behind my only cover, a reception desk less than ten feet from the big guy. I took a breath and lifted an eye and my rifle up just past the desk edge and aimed it at the man. Now I'm going to have to shoot two live ones in the same office. My stomach gurgled at this.

"Blimey," said a voice I recognized. Pecker, one of Buster's men, marched into view. He slid a bandanna he had been wearing over his mouth to his chin and leaned down to inspect the bodies, which I could no longer see.

"Looks like Mole and Blondie were where they shouldn't be," the big guy said.

"They didn't die here, Tiny," Pecker announced.

"Whaddya mean?" the portly man asked, before launching again into another fit of coughing. He must have been sucking in some of the ash.

"They were dumped here in those rugs and staged to look like they were killed by the owner of the insurance agency, as if insurance agents carry a semi-auto rifle around with them while they're hawking life insurance."

"Whatever," Tiny said, while turning toward me—I dropped down below the desk—"Maybe we should see what's in here."

I gritted my teeth, while making myself as small as I could, hoping they didn't see me and I didn't have to shoot. There was a small hole in the metal backing of the desk and I could watch them there, without being seen. Right then, I couldn't remember if the safety was off or not, but I didn't want to take my eyes off these two men to check.

"Ha! You won't find shit here," Pecker said, but his gaze was cast on the floor in my direction. "We got what we came for. We found the boss's truck. Let's go."

"What about these guys?" Tiny asked.

"Leave 'em. Keys are in the truck. I'll drive it and you drive the Range Rover." Pecker handed Tiny some keys and stomped out of the office, banging through the door.

"Oh cool. You never let me... Wait foh me." Tiny waddled out. The door clattered again, and so did the throaty engine of the red Dodge pickup I had left out front.

How did I not get caught?

I let out a long sigh, but then gulped back a breath of dusty air. I had forgotten to remove my belongings from the truck; the boxes of stuff they had stolen from my house were still in the bed of the truck. I wasn't sure what they had taken, and most things were unimportant. But there could have been things inside one of the boxes that pointed to me. I flashed Liz's jewelry box, which was in one of the items they'd taken. Inside it was a gold pendant from me that said "Ron and Liz Ash, forever."

Was that enough to implicate me? Would they come back inside and check again?

I didn't wait to have these questions answered for me: I rose from behind the desk, intending to dash to the exit door, but I halted and so did my heart. All over the carpet were my ash-laden boot prints, leading from the front door to my hiding place. Pecker saw this; that's what he was looking at. He fricking knew I was there. So why didn't he investigate?

My mind wrestled with this at the same time I dashed to the exit door, not even tossing a gaze to the front door—I definitely heard them leave.

My mental resolution was as quick as my scurry out of the office: Pecker must have thought whoever shot his men was still there, unseen, and he didn't want to meet the same fate. So Pecker said out loud, for my benefit, that he was done and why. It totally made sense. But it also meant they might have set a trap for me at the front door.

At the only other door in the office, which I had hoped would lead outside, I cranked the handle, pushed it open and was greeted by a monster-sized dog face.

The beast's paws pummeled my chest, knocking me to the floor.

Just before I hit, I watched it leap at me.

I couldn't turn the gun on it quick enough, so I tried to block it with the gun itself.

But in an instant, it had bounded up and over me, landing its hind paws a mere inch from my head. Then it shot out the damaged front door.

I heard his muffled barks disappear into the distance.

My heart pounded like bongos in my chest and I considered my dumb luck at surviving both the giant dog and Buster's men. Not wanting to press my luck any further, and needing to get out of this place and finish what I set out to do, I hopped back up, fully intending to dash out the back. But I thought about the dog.

That dog must have been Sue Ellen's, and it made sense because I vaguely remembered a whimper behind this door when we met with Sue Ellen. Liz had told me that Sue Ellen kept her dog secured when she ran out for food or had clients over... He must have been there two days, ever since the giant wave. The poor boy must be starving. I was always a sucker for pups; unlike people, they were loyal and always loved you, even when you didn't deserve their love. We just never had one because of Liz's allergies.

I could see the open door led to a room, which then led to another door with an Exit sign above it. My exit.

Instead, I reached into my pack and pulled out the sandwich that Sarah had packed me. My mouth watered when I unwrapped it. But I'd eaten something this morning, while the dog had been without a meal for days.

First I was careful to make sure Pecker and Tiny were definitely gone, before the sandwich was laid on the concrete outside the front door. "Hey, dog!" I yelled and then I whistled. "Here boy. If you're hungry."

I'd done all I could do.

I told myself he'd survive, even though I wasn't so sure. Since I was already outside, I marched my way around the other side of the building and turned toward the river, two blocks away, and stopped.

The river led away from town, and my final stop, but a part of me wanted to continue my search. That part of me did not want to give up on her, no matter how ridiculous the thought was that Liz was still alive.

Then Bob's words rattled in my head: "Don't wait!"

"Screw you, Bob!"

But he was right. I couldn't wait. I needed to finish and get back. I needed to focus on the living, and those who depended on me.

"Fine," I huffed. I turned back to town and sprinted.

Darting from building to building and hanging tight to the shadows, I made my way to my final stop. Well, two stops, actually.

But every so often, I halted abruptly and turned back. It felt like someone was following me. But each time I looked, I saw no one.

On the way to my final stop, I wanted to check on the condition of Randell's, our local grocery store: I was hungry, not to mention curious if there were any more supplies there.

Again, I couldn't shake the nagging feeling of being followed. Yet each time I checked, there was no one there.

When the store I'd been to hundreds of times over the years came into view, my anxiety peaked.

It wasn't the broken windows and obvious water damage that was disturbing, nor that it looked like looters had already hit the place. It was the black Range Rover and red Dodge pickup truck parked in front of it; the same Dodge I'd stolen and purposely parked in front of Sue Ellen's. Pecker and Tiny were coming outside, with their hands loaded with shopping bags full of stuff. My stomach protested this injustice. But I turned away and headed to my last stop a few doors away.

Nanette asked, if I happened to be close, if I could check on her apartment to see if any of it was still there. I thought I'd do a little more than this.

I knew the place well, because a friend of mine used to live next door. But as I stood in front of the brick building, I almost didn't recognize it.

It leaned away from the street at a horrible angle. No longer a sturdy brick building with some history to it, it was a Jenga-like tower of battered pieces, each loosely resting on top of the other, all about to topple over. "Remove just one more brick..."

Upon closer inspection, I could see the back half of the building had already collapsed and much of the second floor and Nanette's apartment had caved in on itself. Cloaked in gray debris, the water-soaked contents of her apartment and probably others were strewn out onto the back alley. It looked like a Halloween pumpkin had broken open and its insides had spilled out everywhere.

Sticking up from the ashes were, of all things, an Etch-a-Sketch. I hadn't seen one of these in years, and I felt compelled to pick it up before continuing to the back of the property.

Halfway around the place, my foot crunched on an object obscured by the ash and mud, its glass cracking. Lifting my foot, I could see it was a picture frame. I snatched it up and shook away the ash and broken glass, revealing a picture of a much younger Nanette, with her arms wrapped around a pale woman, older than her, missing her hair, like she was a cancer patient. "It's your mom," I said to the picture, remembering Nanette telling Sarah that she'd lost her mother to cancer at an early age, and her father a little later.

In front of me was a jarred-open chest of drawers, somewhat covered in bricks and ash. Ladies' underwear and other clothing appeared to be pouring out of it. Another picture of a pretty Nanette and a friend, both in bikinis, was taped to the chest's top. I yanked this one too and slipped both pictures and the Etch-a-Sketch into my pack. Then another thought struck me.

She might also like a few of her own clothes.

Just a little farther in the rubble was a sports bag, with a strap. It was perfect.

I scaled a few feet of jagged bricks and reached into an opening to grab the bag.

At that moment, the bricks under me felt like they were giving way. This was followed by an immediate rumble underneath and all around. I realized it was an another earthquake.

Fear hit and I shot a glance up at what remained of the second-floor wall. It was swaying right above me and I knew what would happen next.

I was too far into the rubble to escape. So I darted for the only place I thought I could survive: the opening where I'd found the bag. It was an opening into a bathroom with a claw-footed bathtub on its side. I barreled into the bathtub, just as the rest of the apartment structure fell on top of me.

CHAPTER 16

Nan

It was like some evil amusement park ride, bouncing us hard upon the ash-covered asphalt.

And unlike my first earthquake experience days before, it was impossible to maintain control during this one. At one point, I was turned over and violently smashed chest-first to the ground. My already-broken ribs screamed with so much pain, I thought I'd pass out. I wanted to close my eyes, but I was also electrified by the scene around me.

Everything seemed to be shaking, and it wasn't just me.

The earth below us turned from a noisy rattle-sound to a grinding sound, as if I were actually hearing two tectonic plates—I'd gotten an "A" in geology class—moving against each other, rock against rock, directly underneath.

"Oh God, no!" Sarah yelped behind me.

I flipped around—more pain—to her, when the grinding sound crescendoed to an explosive cracking sound. And I couldn't believe my eyes.

It was Phyllis and Ethan's home, at the top of the hill we'd just come from, breaking from its moorings on the hillside.

It tumbled in one long, lumbering, slow-motion cartwheel, down the side of the hill...

Toward us.

Sarah's hand clasped hard onto my broken arm and yanked me up, but the ground had other intentions, pulling us both back down.

My eyes remained glued to the tumbling home. Even in its slow rotations downward, it was almost upon us.

Sarah tugged again, this time my other arm, and I really tried to stand up, but I just couldn't get my footing on the crazy-moving surface.

Just before the former home of Phyllis and Ethan rolled on top of us, crushing us out of existence, it made a hard turn and crashed past us, taking out half of another home.

The shaking stopped, but the God-awful cracking and smashing noises continued just a few feet from us, as pieces of two more homes rolled down the hill and into the river below.

My ears rang and my vision blurred, I think more from tears than physical injury. The thought of Phyllis and Ethan, who had no chance and now were gone, added to the soul-crushing realization that they were two more people I knew who were dead. It was an insurmountable weight. So many people were dying or had died. And we had almost joined them, and might still. And worse, all our efforts to help were a complete waste. It was all... so... Hopeless.

The outside air and the ground's death-like coldness sank in. The rest of my own body's heat was drained out, as if the ground was some living heat-vampire intent on draining me of all my life-sustaining warmth. I began to shiver uncontrollably.

"Can..." asked a distant voice.

A viselike grip clasped me. Again it was Sarah, her mask-covered face pressed up against mine, but she seemed farther away. And I was drifting away into the land of despair.

"Can. You. Move?" she hollered her muffled words at me.

"They're dead. They're all dead," I squeaked.

"But we aren't. At least not yet. Get up," she commanded.

"How do we bury everyone? So many are dying... Wh-where will we put all the bodies?" I knew I was talking gibberish. I was half out of it, and the other half was so emotional and nonsensical at that point.

"Let's survive first. We'll worry about the dead bodies after."

Of course, Sarah's words made perfect sense. She was the only one of us who was being sensible at that moment.

But I just didn't care. My mind was overwhelmed with images of all the dead. I was picturing them piling up and nowhere to put them, with the ground freezing over. How would we be able to dig the graves? And how could we wait, if we were starting a new Ice Age, as Sarah was saying?

These were the thoughts of someone who had completely lost it... Someone who had checked out.

That was me.

In spite of Sarah's continued insistence, I just lay there on the ground, shivering from the cold and the loss and the prospect that nothing but death awaited all of us.

But these thoughts didn't last long.

My shivering turned into trembling, interrupted by more grinding noises.

I glanced up to see if Sarah noticed this. Even through her mask, I saw it instantly in her eyes. Shock.

"Oh shit," she said. Then we were falling.

Falling.

And we hit.

Then we both tumbled and flew.

And hit again...

I woke to an icy-cold splash against my face, and water filling my mouth. Then pure panic.

I lifted my head from the water, gasping, and was shocked to see I was at the river.

No, I'm in the river!

At that moment, I couldn't feel anything but my face and I thought that maybe somehow my head was severed from the rest of my body. And there was a roar in my head.

But it wasn't in my head, it was everywhere around my head; it was the river; I had fallen all the way down from the road into the river.

Why can't I feel my arms and legs?

I twisted my head, attempting to glance down. My body was submerged in the water, pinned in a mass of debris: tree branches, a pair of skis, a wheel barrel, a shovel, and more. It was like I landed in a landfill, with a river running through it.

Somehow I pulled my good arm out and pushed on the clog of debris that hung on me.

I'm free!

But I still couldn't feel anything, even though I could see my wrapped arm and legs looked whole. And I was no longer in the river, but beside it. The water coursed around my body.

Then everything moved.

The field of debris I was on lurched forward, farther into the river. I had to get out or I'd be washed away into the raging river, like Ron's Liz.

My free arm and legs didn't work too well, but panic was my assistant. I clawed and kicked and worked my way over the mess of garbage that was everywhere, until I found sold earth. Delightfully cold, hard ground.

A fog of steam billowed out of my mouth, as I huffed and puffed. But I no longer felt cold, which was weird, and all I wanted then was to sleep. I felt so tired, but I knew I had to find Sarah first.

"Sarah?" I trumpeted into the air. But I'm not sure I said anything, because I couldn't even hear my own voice.

There was something just ahead of me, which I knew I had to see. I crawled in that direction, toward it, whatever it was. A dull realization formed in my mind.

It was a woman.

Her eyes were open. Lifeless.

It was Phyllis.

My God, I wanted to scream.

And another dead body was beside her.

"Sarah!" I yelled with every ounce of strength left in me. "Are you alive?"

This I heard.

I pleaded with God that she be still alive. Even though I was no longer the praying type, I prayed right then. I looked up again.

Phyllis gave a dead person's response.

Then I saw movement.

Another form appeared in the distance.

This person was hiking down the hillside.

Coming closer.

Sleep first and then I can look.

My eyes fluttered, but latched onto the approaching face. Was it a face?

It was a black mask, with a white S painted on its forehead.

It was Sarah.

I knew I'd be safe.

At last, I let go and closed my eyes.

CHAPTER 17

Ron

I'd never been buried alive before, so I didn't know how I should feel, other than disoriented. I couldn't tell if I was up or down, much less conscious or unconscious. Conscious, I think.

Are my eyes open?

It felt like they were open, but it was just as black as when they were closed.

One thing was for sure... This wasn't a nightmare: Sharp bites of pain nipped at every part of my body, especially my left leg, alerting me to this reality.

And I was damned hungry.

I don't remember ever starving in a dream or nightmare.

I cursed myself for giving away my sandwich to a dog that probably wouldn't survive a few more days of this. "Dammit!"

Heard that.

My voice sounded muffled, and either water began dripping or I had just noticed this sound; it made me feel like I was buried in a cave.

Time for a systems check.

I may not have been able to see a damned thing, but I could feel. And I needed to check myself for injuries and see what range of motion I had before I attempted to dig myself out of this. It seemed logical and it kept me from panicking.

My left arm was immobile, but that was because I was lying on top of it. My right hand confirmed this and that I was facing the inside of a bathtub. I remembered right then the claw-footed bathtub I had leapt into.

I lifted my hand to my face and felt the foreign goggles and mask, moving both to my neck.

My gasps echoed.

"Holy shit!" I spat.

A heavy mass pressed my lower half into the tub, while I could move my upper half without any trouble. But any attempt at shifting my left leg caused a debilitating shot of pain.

I worked my hand down, starting with my waist, palpating every part on the way down to make sure I was fine. I stopped at my lower leg when I felt a metal rod pushing hard against my calf.

The disorientation is what led me to my next action: I yanked at the metal rod.

Electric flares of agony exploded, and my vision filled with white spots. That was with my eyes closed.

The rod wasn't against my leg; it was in my leg.

"Shit-shit-shit," I yelped, feeling fully deflated. I wasn't sure how I'd make it out of this. I was feeling sleepy, probably from the cold, and the stickiness in my hand meant my leg was bleeding. Even if I could somehow get out of this, if my leg was badly damaged, how would I walk back?

I knew it was bad to even consider, but I allowed myself to nod off.

Barking.

I'm dreaming of a dog.

A louder bark startled my head forward, and a sharp rap against the inside of the tub woke me.

Scratching followed by barking. I was definitely hearing it.

"Hello? Is that you... dog?" I hollered. "Dog!"

It couldn't be. Dog and I had met for only a millisecond, the time it took to knock me down and run off. Was it even possible that Dog was outside my grave of bricks and debris, calling to me? It sounded too crazy to consider. But as I crooked my head back away from the tub, I swore I saw the smallest sliver of light.

Stretching farther and ignoring the pain, I called, "Is that you, Dog? Please help me, boy."

Digging sounds.

My thoughts raced and my mind clamored for hope. I wrestled my other hand free and now could see the faintest of movement from my hands.

Ignoring the burning icicles in my leg, I reached around and swung my backpack forward close enough that I could stick a hand inside.

"Bingo!"

Out came my flashlight. I snapped it on and had to blink back the brightness.

I knew what I needed to do next. I just didn't want to.

Swinging the beam down, and twisting my body to give me a better view in that direction, I could now see what lay ahead for me.

It was a piece of rebar, jammed into my leg. But the good news was that it didn't go all the way through. If I was lucky I might be able pull it out. If I could get some leverage and not pass out in the process.

The scratching stopped, followed by a bark.

"I'm here, Dog. Don't give up on me," I barked back.

The scratching started up again.

I twisted as hard as I could, almost not feeling the pain, or my legs anymore and scanned what was behind me. Then I twisted back the other way and examined the pile of bricks and rebar pressing against my leg. I found my answer.

A baseball bat was wedged just above me, and just outside my tub enclosure. If I could get it, I might be able to use it as a lever, and move the pile of bricks. And then again, I might collapse the whole shit-show down on top of me. I had to try.

One attempt was all it took to snag the bat, and surprisingly it came free easily, almost bonking me in the head with the big end.

Sliding the handle-end of the bat in between the tub edge and a clog of bricks and debris, I pushed as hard as I could, feeling every pound of this unmovable weight.

But then it moved. Or rather I moved. And then I screamed.

I once had an anvil drop on my foot, crushing twenty-three bones and causing me to miss a year of high school. I remembered the pain vividly. This was worse.

I held my breath, grabbed the flashlight from my pit and shined it down to my injury. Blood flowed from the open wound. But I was free.

The bat clattered below and I slid my leg out, then my body, until I was completely out of the tub in an open space.

I yanked a long-sleeved shirt out of my pack and tied it tightly around my leg wound to stem the blood flow. The pressure was painful, but satisfying. Then I saw it.

My rifle. I almost chuckled because it had been right below me and I could have used it instead of the bat. I snagged the strap and tossed it over my shoulder, where I caught movement.

When I clicked off the flashlight, a fuzzy image resolved itself.

It was the maw of Dog. He was just outside of a small hole. The Bull Mastiff's tongue hung out of his jowl and he barked a beefy, satisfied bark.

"Hey Dog. Did you dig that hole?"

Another bark.

I stuck my hand through the hole—it barely fit—and thrust it toward Dog's face. For just a moment, I panicked and considered how stupid this was, because Dog might have been just as likely to see my hand as his next meal. But I felt a slobber-filled tongue brush against me and heard a series of rapid-fire barks. And I was filled with joy.

I withdrew my hand and peeked again through the hole.

Dog had turned away from me. He was looking at something else.

Then he barked once at me and dashed away.

"Dog. Come back," I yelled and then glared again through the hole, no longer seeing my only lifeline to the outside.

I couldn't think of what else to do. So I grabbed a loose brick and used it to dig.

Vigorously I dug, making the hole almost big enough to stick my head through when I had to stop and catch my breath.

Once again, I felt so tired and now weak. I also felt lost.

I allowed my thoughts to fall on Liz. I didn't want to face this world without her. She was my everything. I just couldn't do it.

My vision grew blurry, either from my weakness or my tears, or both.

I sobbed then, thinking of her.

Before I blacked out, I dreamed of Liz floating in the water.

CHAPTER 18

Nan

No panic this time; just a weird combination of agony followed by joy.

It wasn't as dark as when I had woken up in a panic at Ron's place. This time a thin sliver of light beckoned me from across the room. No disorientation: I knew right away this was Bob and Sarah's place... It's just Sarah's now, I thought. With these realizations came the agony.

Every square millimeter of my body felt like it was being stabbed in every way: millions of pins and needles poked at my extremities, and chisels and cleavers hacked at my chest and bundled arm. Oh God, did I hurt. Then it hit me...

I am alive!

However unbelievable it may have been, I survived two impossible situations and woke to face another day. This revelation was an instant salve to my pain, much better than any morphine drip.

I swung out of the bed I was in, without any anxiety this time. I didn't even mind the horrible sulfur smell, which permeated everything, even inside. Something about being alive after everything I'd been through felt like a great gift... from God, my subconscious reminded... "and Sarah," I reminded it back.

At that moment, I needed to thank Sarah for saving me.

How did she save me? I wondered, as I trudged to the doorway; each step was torture.

She was shorter than me and hardly weighed anything, and older. She couldn't have possibly carried me the whole way back up the hill. Could she?

My attention was diverted the moment I turned into the hall.

It was a disaster-scene of busted picture frames and glass. Every picture, but one, had been shaken off the walls—exposed nails and hooks were evidence of this—and onto their tile floor.

The lone picture on the wall, tilting just slightly, was from several years ago: Bob and Sarah standing next to a family, none of whom she recognized. Except one. A lanky boy in the middle, surrounded by what looked like younger siblings. It was Ron, probably high-school age, flashing a broad, toothy smile for the camera, while holding out a model speedboat.

Make a mental note: Ask him about this moment, and about his brother and sisters.

I crunched on tiptoes through the hall and entered their living area, which was a greater catastrophe. I didn't stop though, walking—more so zombie-like lumbering—around an over-turned table and a broken terracotta vase to get to the kitchen. That's where I found Sarah. Sobbing.

It was a stark contrast to the strong, unflappable woman who got things done. The sheer weight of her losses must have caught up with even her. She sat at her kitchen table, head slumped in her hands. She looked small and vulnerable. Her husband was gone, her home tossed and in shambles, her neighborhood almost leveled and so many of her friends dead. And now she was alone.

Well, almost.

I shuffled over to her, biting back my physical pain, to offer whatever small comfort I could.

She obviously heard me, as her head snapped up, face struggling to find its normal rocky features, while she swiftly wiped away her tears. "Looks like the dead have arisen," she croaked.

"Ha!" I said, in an unfamiliar Kathleen-Turner voice. "I do feel like the walking dead."

I put a hand on her shoulder, squeezed and then, feeling like I needed to, I immediately removed it. She didn't appear to want my comfort. So I changed tack. "How in God's name did you drag me all the way back here?"

"I didn't."

"But..." I flashed her an 'I need help with this one' look and sat down in the chair beside her.

She glared at me. A little curl of a smile attempted to appear, but she beat it back and bolted out from her chair. "You were falling asleep, and I knew you'd die if I left you. So I slapped your face and told you that Ronald was waiting for you back at the house. You walked the rest of the way."

My head spun, not so much because I couldn't remember any of this, but because she knew about my attraction to Ron. Under her unrelenting gaze, I felt flushed.

Finally, she turned away, reached down, snatching a backpack, and slung it onto her shoulders. It was then that I also noticed the shotgun on the counter, which she also grabbed.

"Where are you going?"

"To find Ronald." I instantly became worried. "He's been gone far too long and I'm afraid—"

"How long have I been out?" I interrupted.

"A couple of hours. Not long, but Ronald's mission was pretty simple. I'm afraid something happened during the earthquake."

"Okay then, I'm coming too."

"You'll do no such thin—"

"Look," I said, "I'll give you another set of eyes, and I won't leave the vehicle. And if I pass out, better it be with you than alone in this house: don't know who else might come around."

Sarah thought about this, and then nodded. "Your pack is by the door. Come on."

"Pack?"

I didn't know what she meant, but found myself scurrying after her. And by the door was a camouflage backpack, which I guess was my "pack." On top of it was a new set of goggles and a mask to hold back the ash. Those went on first.

The pack was heavy, but I tried to restrain my grunts as I slung it around a shoulder, feeling every pressure point, and I stumbled through the door, pulling it closed behind me.

She had already pulled her SUV out front, and I found myself having to rush to get into the passenger side before she had us moving.

Through wisps of gray ash, Sarah drove fast and steady, while answering my many questions about the packs we were carrying. Each of us surveyed the landscape, looking for any signs of Ron. There were none.

Within a few short minutes we were driving on Main Street headed toward downtown. Even in the murkiness, the scene was terrifying. As we swung off Main onto another street, I turned to Sarah.

"Thank you for saving me."

"You saved yourself, Nanette."

"But it wouldn't have happened without you. So thanks. And I want you to know"—we stopped—"I will do my best to help you and Ron with whatever you need."

"Right now, I need you to grab your revolver from your bag, keep quiet and stay in the truck."

"What am I supposed to do?"

"Nothing. But if you see one of Buster's men approach my truck, blast 'em with your cannon."

With that, Sarah exited the truck, closing the door quietly. She slunk to the back door of Randell's, with the business end of her shotgun raised. She pulled out a key and used it to open the door.

Then she was gone.

My head was reeling with more questions, when I caught movement at the front of the store. A man, pushing and pulling two shopping carts, each filled with groceries.

Sarah had parked us at the back corner of the store, with our front end sticking just barely past the back corner edge of the store. We were forward enough that I saw the man was in a hurry, filling up the bed of a red pickup truck. I could only see the back half of the truck. But it was enough. That's when I was hit with two face-slaps of realization.

It was the same pickup truck driven by the two men Sarah and Bob shot; the same men who had killed Bob; the same two men whose bodies Ron should have disposed of.

And the man filling up the truck was my husband Bud.

CHAPTER 19

Ron

She's not dead after all. She's very much alive and smiling wildly in the mid-afternoon sun. I knew she'd just hooked a big one...

Such a great moment. One of the best in memory.

I'm excited at the size of her catch, and I help her pull it out. The sucker is heavy.

This time, she insists that she wants to clean it herself; I always clean the fish she catches.

Next thing I know she's covered in blood. She says, "Look what I've done, Ronald."

She hands me a rag to clean the blood off her and it's already soaked with her blood.

My hands are now covered in it.

I give the rag back to her and look up for understanding, only it's Nanette now and not Liz. She hands the rag back to me and commands, "Get up."

I don't want the rag: it feels slimy and rough, but she barks again, Rouff-ruff.

I woke to Dog licking my hand like a lollipop, outstretched through the hole of my tomb. I yanked it back and gazed out the opening, my only lifeline to the outside world.

"I'm awake, Dog," I stated, my voice horse and raspy.

Dog barked rapid-fire, then dashed out of sight again.

It was obvious he was trying to tell me something, but I had no idea what that might be.

Once again, the weight of my situation infected my mind: I had little strength left, and not enough to dig myself out; I no longer felt my legs, which meant I'd lost too much body heat; and even if I could get out of this mess, I'd have to walk the two miles to my house to get to safety. Maybe it would be better to join my Liz in death. Maybe I could see her again there, wherever that was.

Dog barked again in the distance.

I blinked at the waning image from my dusty hole, and noticed more ash falling.

But that wasn't all I saw moving.

And then I heard a voice.

It was a man.

An image materialized in the distance. The blurry figure of someone, walking toward me. And Dog in front, leading him.

Dog barked in my direction, and he hopped up and down.

Only then did it hit me. Dog was trying to bring help to me.

"I'm here," I tried to yell, but it didn't come out more than a croak.

I knew what I needed to do.

There was an old iron pipe somewhere. A quick search was all it took before I found it.

The brick I'd used to dig would have a new purpose. With renewed vigor, I banged it against the iron pipe, creating a loud ping-ping-ping sound.

Once more I banged with abandon, followed by thrusting an arm out the hole and waving my hand in wide arcs.

Again: ping-ping-ping, and waving wildly out the hole. And then I checked.

With my face shoved into the hole, I blinked in a vain attempt to unblur what I saw. The man was closer now and he was running right for me.

"I see you," he yelled.

Thank you, Lord!

I banged again, this time as an expression of joy.

A breathless shadow appeared. "Hello, sir. I'm Joey Rancone. Your dog brought me," he said. Dog barked in reply.

"I'm... Ronald," I said in a scratchy, almost imperceptible voice.

"Hey Ronald. Sit tight. I'll have you dug out in no time.

Nan

It was a small pop-pop sound, like bursting bubble wrap.

My focus had been fixated on the back of the red pickup truck, and I was still in shock at the revelation that Bud was working for the local gangster. More so, I was fearful that he would see me or our vehicle while he unloaded their ill-gotten gains from the front of the store.

Upon hearing the pop-pop sound, I flicked my attention toward the door Sarah had entered only a few minutes ago. The sound had came from behind there.

Boom!—That was Sarah's shotgun blast.

I lifted Ron's loaner-cannon, which felt too heavy for just one hand at that moment. Still, I pointed it at the back door, just as it banged open. Sarah burst through at a gallop.

She bounded into the driver's side, slammed a key into the ignition and floored the accelerator, spinning all four wheels on the ash-covered asphalt.

"If anyone comes out that door," she yelled through rapid-fire breaths, "shoot 'em."

We were already rounding the next block before a short man limped out the back door, one hand clutching his bloody leg, fist-pumping with the other and hollering unheard profanities at us.

"I grazed the bastard. He started shooting at me first for no reason," she huffed. "But I got what I came for."

She slowed us at an intersection of the back alley we were on and a residential street. We inched forward, Sarah's head snapping in all directions, looking for what, I didn't know.

Then she accelerated, following another vehicle's recent tire tracks, already partially obstructed by the newest layer of falling ash, before turning down a side street. Then into another alley, and then down another small residential street, and then into another alley, where she squeezed us into a tight easement in between two residences and parked.

I figured she knew what she was doing, so I didn't say a thing. My heart raced so fast, I wasn't sure I could.

"They won't easily track us here, but we're going to wait for a bit, until they return to their pilfering or go home."

"Who was the small guy you shot?" I asked, while my eyes scoured the front and back windows for any movement, other than the floating flakes of gray.

"Don't know. But he'll be walking with a limp for a while."

"Yeah, he didn't look too happy. Are you worried he saw you?"

"Nah. He's not going to remember some old lady."

"I'd remember the person who shot me... What did you need from inside, and how on earth did you get a key for the back door?" I whispered the last part, because she had lowered her window. Then she leaned over me, opened the glove box, and pulled out a pack of cigarettes.

"Gave these up a while ago, but damned if Bob wouldn't leave a pack in the glove box to tempt me. I'm sure he thought he was strengthening my resolve." She looked up and shrugged her shoulders as if to say, "Yeah, makes no sense to me either."

The cigarette lighter popped out—I didn't even notice her doing that—just about the time she had pulled off the cellophane wrapper and slotted a cigarette into her lips. Like a chain-smoker, she lit, drew in a long breath, and let a giant plume of smoke out her window.

"Oh, I missed that more than I realized..." Cough-cough.

"Bob and I have house keys for most of the homes around our neighborhood, and a few outside." She took another lengthy draw on her cigarette.

I had no idea where she was going with this, thinking that she'd forgotten the first part of my question, or chose not to answer.

"One of our neighbors is the manager of Randell's. And he had often spoken about a large food storage area where they kept overstock for their stores." She held up a key ring, a key dangling below it. "This key opens that storage."

A blur of a truck flew by, behind us, followed by the tortured sound of brakes struggling to find traction on the ash-covered road.

Sarah threw the truck into gear, tapped on the pedal, and lurched us forward.

My eyes drilled holes through the back window, but we were out of sight before they returned. "Do you think they saw us?" I asked.

Sarah didn't answer. Her head moved like a frantic lighthouse strobe, attempting to spotlight any threat which might crash into us.

I remained glued to the back. Nothing.

She took us through several more neighborhoods at a measured but rapid pace, when she hit the brakes hard, locking them up and sliding sideways to a stop.

I spun around in my seat and couldn't believe the wholly unexpected scene out the front windshield.

A dog and two men.

One of the men was Ron.

CHAPTER 20

Ron

Is this another nightmare or is it real? I wondered.

A Range Rover had barreled down the road right at us. And although I had only caught a glimpse of it, I would have sworn it was the same Range Rover that Pecker and Tiny had driven to Sue Ellen's insurance office.

Somehow they found me, was all I could think.

We were about to jump out of the way—or rather, Joey was about to yank me out of the way, his arm squeezing tight around my waist—when the vehicle braked hard and slid to a stop only a few yards in front of us.

Dog moved in between us and the vehicle, hackles up, growling his protective warning.

Then I saw who was driving.

Idling in front of us was actually Bob and Sarah's ancient but perfectly preserved Range Rover, a much older version of the one Buster owned. And it was Sarah behind the wheel, her grin obvious, even through the dirty windshield.

"It's okay, boy," I croaked at Dog. "They're friends," I said to Joey, who was struggling to hold me up.

The passenger door sprang open and out popped Nanette, her smile stretched ear to ear.

I thought my vision was truly playing tricks on me, because in spite of Nanette's obvious excitement at seeing us, she looked like she did the morning after the wave. Worse. And so did Sarah. In fact, I would have sworn that both women had been dragged behind the Range Rover the whole way here: There wasn't a square inch of either of them that wasn't covered with bandages, cuts or bruises. She must have just been through another thrashing from the earthquake. Yet she was obviously feeling good enough to show genuine joy.

"Get in quick," Sarah huffed over Nanette, who had already returned to the passenger side. Nanette slammed the door; its window was open. Sarah fixed her attention away from us, her smile gone. "We're going to have company at any moment."

"Thanks, ma'am," Joey said as he helped me into the back of the truck.

"Come on, Dog," I hollered, slapping the seat next to me.

Dog barked once and then jumped in. He sat hard beside and up against me, panting his happiness. Joey followed, slamming the door behind him.

"These are my new friends, Joey and Dog," I said, though the words came out barely as a whisper.

Nanette, still beaming, handed each of us an opened bottle of water and although at first my throat burned and I burst out coughing, I felt instantly refreshed. I poured some in a cupped hand and Dog slurped it out.

"Thanks," I said, my voice already almost sounding normal.

"Shit," Sarah huffed. She threw the truck into gear and jammed the accelerator, slamming our heads back into our seats. I watched Nanette's head track something out the back window, and her expression instantly changed from joy to abject fear.

Sarah slid us around the street corner we'd just walked down. I grabbed Dog with my newly slimed-hand, fearful his massive frame would tumble out of the seat. In truth, Dog pushed down into the seat's cushion with his giant paws, compensating for our turn and my weight, holding both of us up.

Then I saw the red pickup. Again.

We can't seem to get rid of that damn thing.

It fishtailed behind us, and then quickly regained control and closed the distance. Then Buster's newer Range Rover appeared and it pulled up behind the red pickup.

Bang-bang.

"Bud's shooting at us," Nanette announced, and we all slid down into our seats, including Sarah.

Not wanting to expose my head for a look, I glanced into the rearview mirror and saw the dancing image of the red pickup. Someone I didn't know, but Nanette was calling Bud, was hanging out the truck's passenger window, taking aim at us with a handgun.

Sarah swerved around a dead vehicle in the road, as another shot rang out. Her driver's side mirror exploded.

She immediately hard-turned onto another street, the back of the truck doing a long slide, before its tires grabbed hold and they accelerated.

I saw an opportunity to move higher in my seat and peeked out the side then back window. The pickup truck slid sideways, slinging bags of groceries and a couple of boxes of stolen goods—probably some of my things—out from the truck bed and onto the street.

The truck kept spinning until it banged into a stalled vehicle in the street and came to rest.

Buster's Range Rover roared around the now two stalled vehicles, and then turned onto our road. He started gaining on us.

"Turn down there." Joey pointed to a warehouse access road that headed to the river. "I know where we can lose them," he yelled, his drawl less pronounced now, like he had rolled it up and put it away while he was on duty.

I was all the way up in my seat at this point, and I looked up in the rearview mirror and caught Sarah looking to me for confirmation. I nodded.

We slung onto the straight access road Joey had just recommended. "It's a straight shot," he barked, "then make a hard left for the first warehouse."

Sarah hit the gas and hung on the right side of the road in anticipation of the hard left.

Before we turned, Buster's Range Rover swung onto the access road.

We were trusting this stranger that he wouldn't get us trapped. I had thought this was a dead end. I watched Joey as he glared out my side window at the fast-approaching warehouse and then out the back.

Just then I noticed he had my rifle slung around his front. I had forgotten about it completely.

We slid to the side as we turned, but Sarah did a masterful job of course-correcting and getting us back on a straight path again. She was quite the driver.

"Okay, drive right into that first warehouse, but the moment you enter, swing to the right to avoid an I-beam. Again, go straight at it, but only then, immediately swing to the right, and then drive out the rear door."

Sarah did as he said, gunning the engine and pointing our vehicle for the wide opening in the first warehouse. Our lives were in this stranger's hands.

"Hold up just a little; we want the other guy to follow us right in."

Sarah backed off the accelerator, and we slowed.

The pursuing Range Rover drove into view, following our tracks and gaining more distance on us.

Almost at the warehouse entrance, Joey yelled out, "Don't touch your brakes. Get ready to swing to the right."

We shot through the wide open entrance and we were immediately covered in darkness.

"Now, right," he hollered.

Sarah yanked on the wheel, swinging us right, just as the murky image of a giant I-beam held up by a crane came into focus and then sliced past us.

"We would have run right into..." Nanette's voice disappeared under the sound of our brakes.

We flew out the back of the warehouse and spun around to a stop. Part of me wondered if Sarah wasn't actually the female version of James Bond. I'd never seen someone this good at pursuit driving.

We watched the other Range Rover zoom into the warehouse, turn on its headlamps and then crash right into the I-beam we'd just avoided.

We held on for several long breaths, idling, watching for signs of life from the impaled vehicle, the steel I-beam protruding out of it.

The driver's door popped open and a short man staggered out.

Even from this distance I knew who it was.

"It's that the man you shot," Nanette stated, obviously referring to something they'd experienced but hadn't yet told me.

"Yep. Like a damned cockroach that won't die," Sarah mused.

"You shot Ralph 'Pecker' Romero, ma'am?" Joey asked, his drawl fully unfurled. "He's one of the nastiest people I've ever had the misfortune of meeting. He'll be pissed at you, long after he's lowered into his grave."

I understood what Joey meant. The story about how Pecker got his name came to mind: A trucker who had come through town once a week spread rumors at a bar about how Pecker had "a small package." Upon finding this out, Pecker waited in the bar for four straight days, until the truck driver returned. The story went that Pecker whipped out his package, and then told the trucker that it was the last thing the man would see. Then Pecker blinded the trucker with a pool stick. Buster was so impressed with him, Pecker got a new job, and the name.

We watched this same man stumble around the back of Buster's damaged Range Rover, to the other side, where he stopped and glared right at us.

"Come on, Sarah," I said. "Let's get back home. I need you to look at my leg."

We drove away without any further trouble. But I had that image of Pecker's angry gaze stuck in my head. And I knew that this man would make it his life's work to find us and exact his revenge.

CHAPTER 21

Nan

Turned out, it didn't take long for Pecker to find us.

After we had returned with Ron and his new friends to Sarah's place, we tried to "lay low" as Ron called it. Really all we did is sleep for the first two days straight: our bodies desperately needed time to heal. But even that didn't last long.

Turned out, there was way too much work to be done during an apocalypse.

While we slept, Sarah—who had more energy than a big-box store shelf full of batteries—and her newest helper Joey Rancone, the Army Ranger who had saved Ron, took a day to clean up the earthquake damage in the house and basement storage areas. I'm sure Sarah was excited to have Joey's young and strong hands to do things around the house.

During a break, Joey told us a little of his story. He had been on leave, visiting his parents, when the wave hit, destroying his family home and probably killing his parents as well. He'd been searching the town's rubble for survivors when Dog found him and brought him to Ron. Sarah had given him Bob's study to stay in indefinitely, although he resisted at first. "You're part of our family now," Sarah had explained to him. And just like she did with Ron, Sarah began to look at Joey like a son that she and Bob never had.

The next day—the day Pecker's people found us—Sarah and Joey quietly buried Bob's body. I suspect that Sarah did this, in part, so that she didn't have to bother us. But I also suspect it was a privacy thing: She didn't want to lose it anymore in front of us. She wouldn't give any details about the burial, only that she had done this after she had checked in on me in the morning.

Later that morning, I woke up to a small argument between Joey and Sarah. I shuffled out of my room to find out why.

"But you promised, ma'am... I mean Sarah."

On my way out to the kitchen, I noticed Ron was a few steps ahead of me. He must have been stirred from his sleep at the same time as me.

Dog was on Ron's right side, panting. When Dog heard my footsteps, he gulped back his tongue and glared at me, analyzing. Once his dog-noggin calculated that I wasn't a threat, he returned his gaze back to Ron and Sarah.

"You're a nice young man, Joey. But I'm going to ask that you stay out of this... Oh, hello, Ronald... Nanette," Sarah said with quick glances thrown at both of us.

Sarah had been facing Joey, who was standing, but then she turned and moved away from all of us to the other side of the kitchen.

She had a shoulder through the strap of her pack—which she described to me as her BOB or Bug Out Bag

—and that meant she had planned to go into town or further out.

"What's this all about? Where are you going?" Ron demanded and then hobbled over to a counter, taking an edge so that he could rest and face her at the same time. Dog remained glued to his side, parking himself against Ron's leg. Joey remained standing at the little table in the middle of the kitchen, straddling his chair. He looked thankful that someone else had taken up his cause.

"Look Ronald, I'm going out of my mind waiting. I have to investigate that warehouse and if it's as good as I believe it might be, we can't wait any longer or we might lose it to that thug and his cronies."

"What warehouse?" Ron asked, as he tried to suppress a yawn.

"She has a key to a food warehouse; she got it before shooting that squat-looking guy, Pecker," I added.

Sarah flashed me an angry glance that said, I know how to speak for myself, and then returned to Ron. "It's an intermediate storage facility for food and supplies for the Randell's stores. My friend was manager and I believe was killed in the wave. It's set back off the road, so few people would know about it. And I have the key. But I don't think it's smart to wait—"

"Fine!" Ron interrupted. "You, Joey and I will go in my truck—since neither Pecker nor Buster will be looking for it. We'll do recon first, but we'll be loaded for bear, just in case. And if it is what you think it is, we'll go to a place I know where we can get some trucks to move whatever we can grab and bring it back here."

He turned to Joey. "You can drive a truck, can't you?"

"Yes, sir. I received my CDL when I joined the Army."

"That settles it," Sarah stated. "And no worry about the trucks. There should be several there, all parked outside, and the keys inside—which, of course, I have access to."

"Assuming they turn over after having sucked up all that ash from the last few days," Ron answered. "If not, I know where a dozen or so small trucks are parked inside a protected building. We can borrow a couple, load them up and get out before we're found. I only need my rifle and I'm ready." Ron pivoted on a heel and strode toward his room, I assumed to get the rifle Joey had found buried with Ron.

"Wait, sir," Joey interrupted, stopping Ron mid-step.

Joey moved away from the little kitchen table and beat a path into the dining room. "It's right here. I cleaned it while you were resting. It was dirty and I didn't want you to have a malfunction." He held up Ron's rifle proudly and laid it back down on the dining room table.

"I love this young man!" Sarah exclaimed.

"Thank you, ma'a—Sarah," Joey said, his cheeks turning a rosy shade of red.

Joey held up a worn-looking handgun I hadn't seen before. "Are you sure it's all right that I'm using your husband's 1911?"

"He'd want someone who would appreciate it as much as he did." She flashed him a long smile.

"All right then," Sarah proclaimed, as she snatched up her shotgun from the same dining room table and sashayed to the front door. "Are we all ready to go?"

"Um, sorry, but did you forget someone?" I said.

Ron shot me a glance and a grin, as if what I asked was a dumb question. Then he walked over to what must be the ad-hoc gun-cleaning table, shook Joey's hand and slung his weapon.

"Most certainly not," Sarah bellowed from across the room. "Besides, we need someone here to guard the place. And although Joey and I cleaned up the breakage downstairs, I was hoping you'd update our inventory. Oh, and would you please close up the front-door shutter after we leave?"

I didn't answer right away, at first resisting. But I thought about all she said and it made sense. "Okay, that's fine with me. But shouldn't we have some means of communication? I mean, what if someone shows up, or I don't know..."

"Check your BOB. You have a radio packet with a BaoFeng all charged and ready to go, and instructions on how to use it. Tune into 144.150 and we'll do the same. I think it's channel fifty—five zero—on the programmed channels. If you're not sure, just look at the printed radio guide and remember fifty. Okay?"

I assumed BaoFeng was some foreign word meaning radio, so I just nodded and said, "All right."

I marched over to what now appeared to be the gun table. Covering half of it was a spread-out beach towel, and in the middle of that was the revolver Ron had lent me. It sparkled under the light of the oil lantern at the table's center.

"Thanks, Joey!" I trumpeted, as the three of them made themselves busy at their respective areas. Sarah had set up a pack for each of us, with a heavy coat and other protections against the ashfall.

"What's this?" Joey asked, holding up his elaborate mask and goggles.

"That's actually a painting mask and safety goggles, but they're perfect protection against the ash."

"Not to question you, Sarah, but why is this important? It's just ash," Joey asked, still holding the mask and goggles on a fingertip.

"Breathing in the ash will cause all sorts of ailments, and if you get enough of this stuff in your lungs... It's just not good."

That was all Joey needed. He slid both over his head.

"I've been meaning to ask you, Sarah," Ron said, while cinching down the straps of his mask. "How could you possibly know?"

She smiled and then put her gas mask on. "After that night—however long ago that was—when you and Liz had come out to watch the frozen ash come down, Bob researched what was happening and told me what to expect. He bought out the painting masks and safety goggles from the hardware store and told me what to do with them. He even glued the extra mesh to the goggles to keep the ash out of our eyes."

Both Ron and Joey pulled their goggles away from their eyes and inspected Bob's improvements to them.

"Ah, Sarah?" Joey looked up and offered a soft smile, "I'm sorry to question this too, but what does it matter if we get a little ash in our eyes?"

I was wondering the same thing, but kept silent.

"You can actually go blind if you get enough in your eyes, son," she stated. "Can we go now?" she asked.

Both men offered a nod.

When they were ready, they filed out the door.

Ron stopped and looked down at his new companion, who was ready to follow. "Dog, I need you to stay here with Nanette. Protect her like you've protected me."

Dog whimpered, as if he understood everything that Ron was saying, then clawed at the carpet. He definitely didn't agree with Ron's request.

"I know." Ron rubbed the top of Dog's head. It was weird that these two didn't know each other a few days ago, and yet they looked like they'd grown up together. There was a unique bond between them.

The giant animal sat on his haunches, accepting the attention. He barked once at Ron, after receiving a final pat on the head.

Ron squinted at me. It was a compassionate glance that he held onto for a long moment before saying, "You know, Dog's all right. And I can't explain how, but I am sure he won't let anything happen to you."

I nodded acceptance and he flashed a tentative grin, before he opened the door. A putrid sulfur-stench waifed in, and I found myself repressing a gag as Sarah and Joey breezed through. Ron slammed it shut.

Dog remained staring at where Ron had stood, then he cocked his muzzle at an angle, as if listening to confirm his new master had truly left, or was just hanging behind the door.

Ron said something to the others on the other side of the door. But the door's thickness made it impossible to hear him.

I had already made my way to the door, and once there, I peeked out the peep hole. Sarah and Joey were standing in the cul-de-sac, in front of the house. They were wearing heavy coats, but were already beating warmth into their arms and puffing out plumes of vapor from their masks. It looked really cold out.

"Well, it's just you and me," I told Dog, who was still staring at the door. He was pining for Ron's return.

All at once, I felt alone and exhausted. Even though I had just woken up after sleeping for more than an entire day, I felt like I could sleep for many more days. Sarah had already instructed me on how to seal up the house. I thought I would do that, then read about how to work the radio, and then maybe sleep some more. I really did want to work on the inventory, but sleep felt like a bigger priority.

There was a rumble of a truck outside, which I assumed was Ron's.

Dog crooked his head again and bored holes into the door, like he had x-ray vision too. But when the truck's engine disappeared, Dog groaned and then laid down his massive body onto the carpet, still pointed at the door. He looked ready for sleep too.

My own BOB had been left beside the door, and inside was the radio package. Maybe I'll take my BOB to bed, really look through it and learn what I can about the radio. But at that moment, the weight of the gun, clutched in my left hand, felt really heavy. And every aching bone and muscle in my body had once more begun singing their constant chorus of agony.

The hell with this. I was going to take one of Sarah's pain pills and just go to sleep. Everything else could wait.

Except closing the window shutters.

I stepped away from the door, intending to go to the downstairs entrance, where the bank of switches was located to operate the rolling shutters. I halted when I heard the noise of a truck approach.

I wondered what Ron and Sarah had forgotten, but then Dog started growling.

Dog rose to a stand and growled some more.

I knew then it wasn't Ron.

CHAPTER 22

Ron

It was eerily quiet out, like after a snowfall... but without the color.

The ash had stopped falling. But what was left was a layer of gray coating everything, making it hard to tell where the ground ended and the sky's ashen clouds began. All color had been neutered from the landscape: trees, plants, lawns, even Mrs. Grayson's pink Cadillac—still parked in her driveway—had been shrouded in a gray veil.

Ash crunched below my '78 Ford F250's oversized wheels. Its popping sounds were much too loud for our attempts at being covert. So at first, we had moved from our neighborhood slowly, with our headlights off, silent but for the crinkle of our clothing. Mostly, we didn't want to run into Pecker, Buster or any of his gang, on the off chance they were looking for us. I was holding out hope that Pecker would just die from the injuries he sustained from Sarah's shotgun blast to the knee, and that Buster would ignore us. I guess I was still holding onto hope, where none existed, just like Liz at that point. But I needed to let go of hope, just like I needed to let go of Liz.

We were all anxious about this mission, about running into Buster or his crew, or just regular survivors at this point. It had been five days since the wave had wiped out most of the people who lived in our little town. Then another earthquake did in a bunch more. Bob had told me that most people have a single week's food supply on hand—two weeks at the most. I suspected the few survivors were probably starting to get desperate now. So we had to be extra careful.

It was also cold out, and my truck didn't have a heater. Even if it did, I was fearful to turn it on and suck up the ash. So to keep the windows from fogging up too badly, I had to have our side windows opened a crack. Joey and Sarah blew heat into their hands in back, which was hard through their masks, adding to the cab's moisture.

When we had turned onto the main road and figured it was okay to go faster, two headlights glared through the windshield. Someone had just turned onto the same street and was now headed toward us, just a few blocks away.

I quickly swerved into another residential street and barreled up a random driveway, out of sight from the road. I spun us around, to allow for a quick getaway if needed, and flicked off the ignition.

"Get down," I whispered, though the command felt silly since we couldn't see the road while we were sitting up, and certainly no one could hear us.

I cracked down my window further and we all listened. We were all panting, like Dog would have been if he'd been here.

The sound of a throaty engine approached, slowed down and then continued on.

"You don't think that was..." Sarah muttered.

I sat up high in my seat. "No."

When I couldn't hear the vehicle anymore, I fired up the truck. "I'm going. Don't think we have much time."

We drove faster, caring less about the noise and more about getting to our destination. But we still scoured the landscape for any signs of other vehicles.

We saw three other vehicles on the way to the warehouse: We were in agreement that Pecker had sent out search parties to look for us. Absence of information fueled our conspiracy theories, and our anxiety.

Somehow we made it to the warehouse without being seen. Or so we thought.

Our target was at the end of a cluster of three massive buildings. The closest end building was Green Growers, which was a medical marijuana grower. I'd always suspected it was owned by Buster and his group of thugs. So I felt especially cautious as we drove past the long building, keeping our speed down, searching and listening for any activity aside from our own. Both side windows remained cracked open, even though it was ice-cold outside and in.

"I don't see any movement there," said Sarah.

"Yeah, we might be in luck," I said.

"Go to the back and let me out," she said.

I eyed a group of trucks parked farther in back, and I could see Joey looking at them, as well.

We pulled in back of the massive warehouse and Sarah hopped out.

"Joey, could you go with Sarah, while I park the truck?"

He nodded and jumped out, the 1911 held down by his side. He calmly pulled the slide back, and flicked off the safety. My stomach was doing full somersaults at this point, as he followed Sarah inside.

Knowing this warehouse complex pretty well—I had looked at it when it was first built for my then-future workshop—I parked in a back parking space, where we wouldn't be easily seen. It was pointed toward an exit for a quick getaway.

I had a perfect view of the back door of the warehouse, and saw that Sarah had wedged it open slightly for my entry. I pulled the wedge out and let it click closed. The warehouse was shrouded in complete darkness, but for the two dancing flashlights moving farther away in the distance. Every second or two, Sarah or Joey would say, "Holy shit" or "Oh my God." I turned on my own flashlight, shot the beam in their direction, and immediately saw why.

CHAPTER 23

Nan

Pound-pound-pound!

I gasped, frozen in place. Dog growled even louder. Too loud?

Pound-pound-pound!

I shot a glance at the oil lamp and cursed that it was still on. Even though whomever was outside couldn't see anything through their side of the eyepiece in the door, they could probably see the dancing light coming from inside, proving someone was home... If they looked.

I made a quick decision: laying my gun down, I flopped my hand over the eye-piece and waited.

My heart beat rapid-fire and I sucked down my breath, while I listened to the muffled quiet outside.

But I couldn't help it. I had to look.

The instant I removed my hand from the eyepiece, my eye was there, staring through it.

An oak-tree-sized man stepped away from the door and said something to another, familiar-looking man, who was turned away and facing the street. They both wore colored bandannas around their faces, like modern-day bank robbers.

What do they want?

A wave of panic raced through me and crescendoed the moment I confirmed why they were here.

Parked in front of the house, on the street, was a red Dodge pickup truck. The same pickup truck that had been in Ron's driveway, then later in front of Randell's, and then chasing us. It had the dents to confirm it was the same one that crashed into the stalled car.

And now, it was in front of Sarah's house.

But how?

The familiar-looking man turned to face the door, and me. He pulled down his bandanna.

My heart galloped. I'd forgotten how to breathe. All I could do was just stare at this man's mug, which I knew so well.

It was my husband, Bud.

"How the hell did you find me?" I whispered at him.

Bud wasn't the brightest bulb in the pack, but maybe the people he worked for were.

His mouth moved and I scoffed that the one time I cared about what he was saying was when I couldn't hear him.

And then I remembered the intercom. Sarah had told me which button to push after Phyllis had been banging on the door for help.

My hand hesitated over the box with several multi-colored buttons. I wanted to be sure I pressed the right one, and not one that would allow them to hear me speaking, or rather breathing wildly.

My finger poked a button and again I gulped back my breath. But I exhaled when crackly voices erupted through the small speaker.

"So what do you want to do?" asked the giant man. "Maybe it was just someone who was casing this neighborhood, like us."

"Maybe. Maybe not. But this is in our grid and if we don't completely check it out, and they're here... Pecker will have our asses. Plus, I think I saw tracks go to their garage..." Bud's head snapped in one direction and then the other: It was a comical rendition of a man pretending to act important when he knew he wasn't.

That's when a thought struck me. How in the hell did I stick with this buffoon for so long?

"You stay here, Tiny," drawled Bud. "I'm going around to the garage and see what's what."

Tiny didn't even acknowledge, looking bored.

I watched my scumbag-husband turn, like his shoulders were bigger than they actually were. He always did this when he lifted weights for a couple of days, thinking he had magically built up his muscles in two sessions of lifting. But just as quickly, he'd lose interest, giving it up because it was too much work.

I held back my snickers; at least my amusement was tamping down my anxiety.

Dog growled some more.

"Shhh, Dog," I said, holding my hand back over the eyepiece. "That stupid man can't hurt us."

That seemed good enough for dog, who sat but remained on alert.

I peered back through. Bud rubbed his hands together, as if to keep warm, but he was only wearing a

T-shirt, which was pretty stupid. Then he abruptly darted in the direction of the garage, tripping over a planter on his way along that side of the house.

I threw my bicep over my mouth to muffle my laughter.

But then I panicked again.

Had Sarah locked the garage door after she parked us? I wondered, sending my glare in that direction. Bud had told me how easy it was to break into a garage from the outside, using just a coat hanger, since most people didn't have any other locking mechanism on the door, like Sarah did. But she was worried about Ron's leg. I don't remember her deploying her lock after shutting the door. "Oh shit!" I huffed, sure that she didn't.

Dog took off, blazing a trail to the garage, barking the whole way. I snatched up the gun and followed, ignoring the pain each abrupt movement caused me. I had to get there before Bud did.

Dog and I held up at the interior garage entrance.

I clanked against the door handle with gun in hand, cursing my useless arm. Sliding Ron's heavy pistol in between my chest and my broken arm, I cracked open the door and Dog burst through.

We were too late.

The garage door was open two feet above the concrete and Bud was already ducking under, one shoulder and butt-cheek first.

Dog was lightning fast, getting to him in half a bark, and burying his teeth into the first substantial thing he could grab: Bud's rear end.

In the dim light, it was hard to see clearly. And I so wished I could have seen Bud's face. My ears filled in the missing images.

Bud let out a soprano-pitched scream, as Dog tore into him, knocking him to the ground.

Bud kicked wildly and screeched like a girl, as he desperately tried to get back out from where he'd come in. But Dog wouldn't let go. He had hold of Bud's rear end.

And at that moment, I became sure Dog would not have let go until after he'd killed Bud. And for some strange reason—maybe nine years of being married to the fool—I felt a little sorry for him. Plus, I was fearful that his carrying on would bring his giant partner.

"Out!" I yelled. "Good Dog."

Dog released him and Bud waddled away, disappearing from sight.

"Come on, Dog. Good boy," I coaxed him back in the garage.

A wire hanger with a hook hung over the top of the door. I leaped up and snagged this and then threw my weight onto the long garage door itself, pushing it to the ground. My ribs and muscles screamed profanities at me. But the door was down.

A quick scan with barely enough light coming from the rear door to show me the lock where I remembered Sarah engaging it the first time. Luckily it was easy, and the bolt slammed home.

"No one's getting in now, boy," I huffed to Dog. He sat on his haunches, panting and waiting for a bigger show of appreciation from me for saving the day. But there wasn't time.

I ran to where Sarah kept a flashlight—she had one in every room now—and clicked it on. I flashed the entire span of the door again, breathing a huge sigh of relief, flooding with light the area Dog had snagged Bud. It was bloody.

"Hope you get an infection," I yelled at no one.

This silly emotional retort would have normally felt good—assuming normal existed anymore—but my anxiety was in high gear. It wasn't just Bud or even Tiny that we had to worry about now; Bud was part of this nefarious group, led by Buster and his henchmen, like Pecker. And they were in fact looking for Sarah and maybe Ron. I had to warn them, and I had to do it now.

I remembered the radio in my pack.

It was a race through the garage entrance, into the kitchen, and to my so-called BOB, perched by the front door.

A quick glance through the peephole confirmed that the huge man was still there. He was shifting from one foot to the other, combating boredom and the cold. No sign of Bud yet, so I focused on the bag.

Near the top was a clear plastic case, with what I suspected was the radio. Clicking it open, I found two radios, each with a multitude of buttons, nested on top of instructions, along with a separate antenna and other stuff.

It looked so much more complicated than I had hoped.

Knowing this was going to take a while, I glanced back out the peephole and sucked in a breath when Bud appeared.

Once again, I punched the intercom receive button and heard the big guy speaking. "... did you find... what happened?"

"God-damned dog bit the shit out of me. I need a doctor," he blubbered, while he continued his hop-lurch and clutched his backside.

"So there is someone here. Did you see if it was the Range Rover we're looking for?"

"Don't know," Bud whimpered, "didn't you hear me? I need to go to the hospital."

"But you did say there were tracks leading into the garage?"

"I feel dizzy. Look, dammit, I'm bleeding!" he screeched and then duck-walked to the truck.

"I'll call it in," Tiny said, completely unconcerned with Bud's injuries, which looked substantial, based on the trail of blood he was leaving behind him.

Tiny snatched what looked like a radio from his side and his beefy thumb and forefinger twisted a dial on the top, causing the light on the screen to flash Tiny, and a computerized female voice said, "Frequency mode." He glared at Bud and yelled, "What frequency again?"

"Ah, 154-something. How the hell... Please, let's go!"

"Geez," I whispered, "put both of you together and you almost have one brain."

"Point-four-five!" Tiny exclaimed, nodding at his recollection. He punched in the number and then pressed a button on the side and said, "Base, this is Tiny."

"Go ahead," crackled the radio.

"Me and Bud are in the field. We have a possible location. We are... Hang on."

"Skip that! Boss wants everyone to go to the Randell's warehouse, next door to Green Growers. On the double."

Tiny looked over to Bud, who was hunkered down by the truck.

"That's where..." Bud yelled "...the boss grows his pot for the dispensaries. Good shit—Come on, let's go." Bud removed a bloody hand from his rump and struggled with the truck door, which appeared hard to open because of the damage from the collision.

Tiny held the radio to his face, and shuffled away from me. "Ah, copy. We're off..."

I watched them both climb into the truck and zoom away. And then it clicked in my brain... Randell's warehouse next to Green Growers.

"Oh shit!" I yelled at the door.

I had to figure out this radio right away, because they were headed to the same warehouse where Ron, Sarah, and Joey were probably already inside, with no idea they were about to be besieged by all of Buster's men.

I had to warn them.

I twisted the round button on top of the radio, just like Tiny did, and likewise the display flashed Nan and then two sets of numbers. Tiny had punched in the frequency 154.45. But that was their frequency. I needed the one that would reach Ron and Sarah.

Out of the plastic box that held the radio was a folded page, titled Radio Guide & Signal Chart, with images and instructions on working the radio and lists of frequencies. Near the top of the page were four "Primary Frequencies" and so I started with the first one, punching it in the display and clicking the same transmit button that Tiny did.

"Hello. I'm looking for Sarah. Sarah, this is Nan... Ah, they are headed your way. Repeat, the bad guys know where you are and are headed to you..."

CHAPTER 24

Ron

I t was bigger than a Costco: floor-to-ceiling shelves of food and other supplies, as far as my flashlight beam would go. And it all appeared to be untouched since the wave.

I couldn't help but smile. There were years upon years' worth of food here. Enough to feed all the survivors of this area many times over. And it was unmolested. If we could just get a small portion of it into our trucks and then into our two homes, we'd be set for however long this thing lasted. We'd worry about finding space for it, or as much of it as we could, after we got it there.

I had resolved that it wasn't stealing. If this apocalypse thing didn't actually turn out as bad as Bob thought it would, I'd pay for whatever we took. I'd leave a note for the owners. Assuming any of them were still alive.

But none of this would happen if we didn't get to it before Buster and his gang found out about this stash and stole everything. And with Green Growers so close, and the prospect of one of Buster's crew seeing us, we'd have to be stealthy and quick.

Sarah and Joey were already spread out, their beams dancing around opposite corners of the warehouse. Sarah was the farthest, her light finding a small office to the right of the front entrance, on the other side of the warehouse. The roar of a diesel engine confirmed Joey had found and started up a forklift near the loading docks to my left. He threw it into gear and raced toward Sarah. I did too.

On the way, I was doing a visual scan of what supplies were located in my aisle, and I came to a halt about midway.

It was an area of prepper supplies including, of all things, gas masks for dogs. I didn't hesitate; I grabbed the largest one and slung it around my other shoulder before continuing.

I arrived at the little office—its placard on the door announced "Warehouse Manager"—just as Sarah exited with a handful of keys and a coy grin. Joey pulled up to us with the forklift and instructed, "Get in."

Sarah emptied her haul into my hands, while Joey put our ride into gear. Racing to the same back exit we'd entered, he kept his eyes forward while offering verbal instructions to Sarah on the forklift's operations. She had said she was rusty, just needing a refresher on the controls. She nodded the whole way.

It was obvious that each of us felt the same sense of urgency. Still, Sarah offered one last bit of instruction. "I'm going to open a couple of loading dock doors, do a quick inventory and then start grabbing food," she yelled over the forklift's engine. "Go get us two trucks, so we can start loading. And please hurry."

Joey screeched us to a stop. We hopped off and trotted out the door, this time not worrying about propping the door back open for our return. Sarah was going to take care of that.

I had thought this through when I had found a place to park my own vehicle. There were at least a dozen box trucks in the warehouse back lot. The trucks closest to the loading docks appeared to have had tire tracks leading up to them. I reasoned that they had been parked there after the first ash had fallen and were therefore less likely to start or even run for long. So I led us to the farthest two trucks and found the two corresponding keys for them. "Let's try these two first," I announced.

Joey nodded, took a key and dashed to his truck. I did the same.

Within a minute, we were both inside, had our trucks started and we were on the move.

It all seemed easy. Too easy.

A part of me wondered if I shouldn't drive up to the front and make sure our coast was clear, but I figured we were all in and there was no time to waste. So I followed Joey to one of the only two open loading bays.

Joey appeared to also be expert at maneuvering trucks, because he was already backed up to the first loading dock. He was inside, when I was backing up to the second loading dock.

I found Sarah giving instructions to Joey, when I approached them.

"I was able to grab one pallet. After you load that, get more. We're going for the long-term food first: canned meat and vegetables, which is down this aisle"—she pointed to the next aisle over on the left from where we stood—"Stay away from the soups. We'll make our own; liquid takes up too much room..."

I marveled at this woman, who I thought was at least seventy. I had not given Sarah much consideration in all these years. Before all of this, I had thought of her as just a kindly retired nurse and avid cruciverbalist, who put up with a lot of crap from her husband Bob. She was so much more.

"Oh Ron"—She'd directed her attention to me now —"I'm a third of the way inventorying the warehouse; can you run over to the front middle and work your way back to me, making a mental note of everything? I'm especially interested in bags of rice and beans, and any prepper or long-term storage foods."

I didn't hesitate, doing exactly as she had instructed, and I ran straight to the front of the warehouse, my flashlight bathing the shelves with light, working each back and forth, looking for what she had asked.

At the very front of the warehouse was a double-door entrance, framed by the manager's office on the right and a couple of vending machines on the left. I'd planned to make a turn there and work my way back down the next aisle, but something caught my attention. It looked like a splash of light on one of the two small window panes inset on each door. I held up and stuck my head up against the pane of the left-most door.

Movement.

I flicked off my light to be sure it wasn't me casting the reflection or causing the movement.

It wasn't.

Through the front door limped Pecker and several other of Buster's men.

My heart sank. We were too late. They had found the place.

And now they were headed right for me.

I pivoted back to the warehouse and blared three sharp whistles. Then I flashed S-O-S at the ceiling, turned off my beam and ran for cover behind a cola machine.

I clung to darkness, feeling a little relief that my message got through to them: Joey cut the forklift's engines and headlights and Sarah's flashlight went dark.

Then I cursed myself for leaving my rifle in the truck. Because our situation had felt safe, I wanted to free up my hands, worried it would get in the way. I wouldn't do that again.

Assuming I even had that chance.

The double doors burst open and I slunk completely behind the soda machine.

"Holy shit, would you look at this," proclaimed an unfamiliar male voice.

"Yeah-yeah," responded another—It was Pecker —"but where are we on finding that bitch who shot me, and her friends?"

"We have a couple of possibilities, and we haven't heard yet from three patrols—" A chirp on a radio interrupted the man speaking.

"I'm here boss," said Pecker. Then his radio beeped.

The radio blared back, "What's the warehouse look like?"

It was Buster.

"Just as I suspected, sir. It's full of food and supplies. At least a year's worth for all of our men."

"Great work tracking this down from Randell's. Now, let's get it secured. Use everyone. This is the priority...Do you copy?"

Pecker's radio chirped again, but nothing was said in reply.

"Got it, sir," Pecker finally huffed. "Over and out."

"Fauuuuk!" Pecker yelled, followed by a loud bang against something metallic.

"All right, fine..." Pecker said in a measured tone. "Call in the rest of the boys, and do what the boss says. I'm going to check this place out."

"Shit," I said under my breath. I peeked past my cover and saw Pecker hobbling away from me. He was headed in Sarah's direction, or at least where I last saw her flashlight.

It might be my only opportunity. So I broke for an opposite corner, the stitches in my leg yanking, and then toward the back where I hoped to find Joey.

He was already by the loading dock exit, waving his arms at me.

"What is it, sir? I saw your message," he asked.

"Buster's crew is here. We have to leave. Where's Sarah?"

"I don't know. Maybe outside?"

"Let's hope she is. We need to go," I said, turning to the door.

It was what we agreed to do: leave the warehouse and meet up outside if someone else entered.

After grabbing my rifle from the truck—I would be sure to sleep with the damned thing from now on—I pulled out my radio and flipped it on, intending to call Sarah.

"—trapped..."—It was Sarah whispering—"Repeat, I'm trapped in the warehouse. And someone is headed right for me. Gotta go—"

CHAPTER 25

Ron

"So our only options are to wait or go back in, guns blazing, and get Sarah..." I huffed, while I limp-paced over the same spot, doing my best to ignore the throbbing pain in my right calf.

The radio was set on a low crackle so we could hear Sarah if she called again. We didn't expect this, though, as we assumed she was still hiding... or worse, she had been captured.

Joey kept his eyes fixed on his feet, rubbing furrows into his temples.

I continued, "But neither of us has been in a gun battle, and one of us is bound to get hurt or worse..."

Joey's head popped up and he glared at me—I wondered if I said something he took wrong. Then he looked up and around from where we were hunkered behind the warehouse, beside an overflowing and very fragrant dumpster.

Before he could say what he had in mind, my radio chirped and both of us held our collective breath.

"Attention Ron and Sarah. This is Nan. The bad guys are headed your way. The bad guys are headed your way. Get out!"

I abruptly clicked the talk button. "Nanette, it's Ron."

"Oh, thank God. You have to be careful. I think..."

I didn't even try to interrupt her. Instead I clicked my microphone button multiple times, and continued to click it for almost a minute to block out anything she might say that could have given away any of our positions.

When I stopped, the radio was silent.

"Please stay off the radio. It's public, and anyone can hear you. And yes, we know about what's coming. Are you all right?"

"Yes... Ah, sorry. I didn't know... I'm fine, but my ex-husband"—she snickered—"is not going to be sitting down for a while. Your dog took a bite out of his south-bound quarters."

"I'll call you back later. Hang tight," I said, not really wanting to ask what she meant about her ex-husband. I probably should be concerned, but...

"Do you still have the other truck keys?" Joey interrupted my mental meanderings. I glanced at him. It was obvious he had something in mind.

"Yes, of course." I said, patting the bulge in my velcroed calf-side pocket.

"Let me have them. I have an idea, sir."

"Here, Joey." I handed him the whole mess of truck keys, hoping he'd fill me in on his plan. "And please call me Ronald."

"Okay... Ronald... I'm going to create a diversion so you can get Sarah out. I'll find a way back to your home."

"Wait, I can't leave you here."

"Sir, I mean Ronald, you'll have a hard enough time getting out of here with Sarah. Let me draw them away from you. After all you all have done, it's the least I could do." He looked at me, and even though we were both hanging in the shadows of this dreary day, I could see he was emotional about this.

"Okay, but take this." I held out my radio, but he wouldn't take it from me.

Instead he clutched my wrist and said, "Thank you, Ronald. But if I lose the radio or worse, get caught, they can tell what frequencies you use. And I don't want to compromise your position. You'd better hold onto that."

"All right," I said. "But please be careful, and find your way back to us. I want the opportunity to pay you back for saving my bacon."

"Copy that, sir." He turned and was about to leave, but he spun back to face me. "When you hear the loud noise, pull up to the loading bay and honk your horn. Sarah will figure it out. She's one of the smartest woman I've ever had the pleasure of meeting. And please take care of her..." He hesitated, "and tell her thank you."

"Copy that," I said.

He ran off, keeping close to the border wall of the property.

My leg throbbed so bad, I momentarily considered sitting down on the ground. But I had to get into position. For Sarah, and for Joey.

Maybe a minute later, about the time I made it to my trusty '78 Ford, I heard a large truck engine start up. My attention was then drawn to the opposite direction:

Coming from the access road, there were multiple headlights approaching the front of the warehouse.

Including the men we'd already seen, this place was about to get really busy.

My always dependable truck almost didn't start, lumbering much longer through its start-up routine than I ever remembered. I could almost feel the ash abrading all of her previously well-tuned parts.

But once I got it going, I turned around and drove toward where Joey had just been to get a look at what he intended. I caught the blurry movement of his box truck—or rather decoy—on the far side of the property. He seemed to be idling, waiting for the right time.

I swung back to the warehouse, pulling up in front of the box truck I had just backed into the loading bay. With my windows rolled down, I stared through the passenger side, into the two dark open bays of the warehouse, while listening for Joey's sign.

I didn't have to wait long.

Somewhere near the front of the warehouse, just seconds after the accelerator of a throaty diesel engine was opened up wide, there was a crashing sound of metal against metal. Then another, and then another. I pictured Joey roaring his box truck through the parking lot, taking out one vehicle after another.

But I had expected something more. Something... louder. And I wondered if that was all there was to his decoy, or if there would be more. I was about to lay into the horn anyway, when I heard the real decoy sound he had spoken about.

A huge whoosh, followed by a deep boom sounded. I swear my truck shook slightly from the blast's percussion. I spun around in my seat to see.

A fiery mushroom blossomed from where the trucks were parked, lighting the darkness.

Then another boom, this one out front, along with the gunfire. Lots of gunfire.

"Shit brother, I hope you make it to tell me what you just did," I said to the windshield and plunged my fist hard into my steering column, blaring the horn.

I had cracked my door open, thinking I would go and get Sarah myself, when a silhouette appeared in the loading bay.

But was it her?

I softly closed my door and lifted my rifle.

The slight figure jumped down with the agility of someone a lot younger than seventy. Then the figure darted for my truck.

My rifle now leveled, the red dot plainly painted on the approaching figure, I clicked off the safety. With the person clearly sighted in, I felt that dread seep into my gut once again, knowing what I had to do next... if this wasn't Sarah.

I huffed out a long breath, pulled my eye away from the sight and flicked on the safety.

Sarah jumped in, hyperventilating.

At the same time, I gassed it and we jumped from our position. We headed down a path I'd mentally carved out, through the back-side of the warehouses.

"Was that our Joey who made the explosions?" she asked.

At first I smiled my answer, but then plunged on the brake pedal, bringing us to a stop at the drive to the front parking area, right in between this warehouse and the next one. We both glared out the passenger-side window.

Our eyes had trouble keeping up with all of the vehicles and men dashing in random directions. It was chaos.

Then we saw him.

A lone figure, running away from Randell's warehouse, being chased down by two vehicles: a small car and an SUV.

"Joey!" screamed Sarah.

My mind screamed too, and I stomped on the accelerator, screeching our tires, wrestling with the steering to keep us turned toward Joey and the front of the warehouses. We raced in between Randell's and Green Growers, as I aimed for the lead pursuit vehicle, not at all sure I could get there in time.

We roared out from the back of the warehouse parking lot onto the front and I only caught a glimpse of the truck and three cars on fire.

"Oh my," said Sarah as we fast approached the two vehicles trying to run down our new friend. But I realized right away, I wasn't going to make it in time.

What looked like a Mini-Cooper gunned past a lone parked car, hopped up a curb and plowed into Joey, sending him end over end. Sarah shrieked when he landed in front of the parked car, out of sight.

The second vehicle, an SUV, swung too far, hit its brakes and screeched to a stop on the other side of the parked vehicle, while the Mini-Cooper spun around and gunned its hot-rod engine, obviously intending to finish Joey off. I didn't give him a chance.

Even in the low-light conditions, I could see the driver's face: a man whose vacant eyes were screwed onto his target, licking his lips in anticipation of the death he couldn't wait to inflict.

Just before I hit him, he glanced up, not expecting me, and his face turned satisfyingly terrified.

My truck is a Ford F-250 Diesel, weighing in at six thousand pounds. When we struck the little Mini-Cooper, it crinkled like an empty aluminum soda can, which then flattened even more after I drove through and then over it.

My foot found the brakes and we slid to a halt. I spun back in my seat to look at what was left of the car we had destroyed and to find Joey.

"Ronald!" screamed Sarah.

I turned to her side and saw it right away. The SUV had a new target: It was coming directly at us from Sarah's side.

Its brights bore down on us, its engine whining. At the last moment, with Sarah wiggling in her seat, ready to burst out of the truck, I threw us into reverse and jammed the accelerator.

The driver didn't expect this, as I backed up over the flattened Mini-Cooper and its equally compressed driver. The SUV was about to plow through empty space where we had been and, I had hoped, the parked car beside us.

But I was just a moment too slow.

The SUV corrected just enough to clip my front quarter-panel and spin us around like a carnival ride.

Sarah shrieked and I think I did as well, as we rotated around at least once.

When we came to rest, the SUV had already spun itself around and was now directly facing us. Its front end was shredded open, like the ragged maw of a rabid dog. Its windshield, still intact but cracked into a thousand diamonds, reflected the spreading fire in front of the warehouse like a single evil eye. Its growling engine was revved over and over again. This junkyard dog was challenging us to a game of chicken.

I didn't intend to play, throwing us into second, intending to drive behind the parked car and lead him away from wherever Joey was.

But we were stuck.

What was left of the crumpled Mini-Cooper was now wedged underneath us, keeping our two back tires off the pavement. I tried to rock it by shifting back and forth, but it wouldn't budge.

The SUV rocketed forward, sensing the easy kill.

Its engine thundered at an abnormally high RPM, and the driver gunned for me, his high beams both blinding and painting his target.

Realizing the futility of our situation, I reached for my rifle, when a figure jumped in front of me. This silhouette cut back the headlights enough that I saw him raise a pistol—or more specifically a 1911—take aim and fire.

Boom-boom-boom-boom-boom-boom-boom.

The percussion, right outside my window, was very loud and I swore my eardrums shattered again. Yet I was entirely focused on Joey, highlighted by the oncoming headlights. His slide was all the way back of his emptied weapon. He wobbled and then fell to the ground.

The SUV swerved once. And then a second time. It swept past us and into the parked car beside me. The crashing sound was a dull thud, as church bells continued to ring in my ears.

"Joey!" yelled Sarah—again dull, like I was wearing ear muffs.

Sarah was out her door and was first to him. I hopped out, slinging my rifle to my chest.

Even in the darkened haze, I could see Joey was in bad shape. He was a mass of blood and misshapen limbs.

"He's still alive!" Sarah announced.

I scanned the parking lot and was surprised that no one else was around. They were all buzzing around the front of the warehouse. "Let's get Joey and you in the truck bed. We need to get out of here."

She nodded and we hoisted Joey to the back bumper. "Hold up here," I said, leaving them. I had remembered seeing a good-sized tree limb on the other side of the stalled car. It should be perfect. I dashed over, found it, and dragged it across the pavement, holding up beside the SUV.

I couldn't believe my eyes.

The SUV looked familiar enough: It was a brand new Range Rover, just like the one that crashed after pursuing us. And in the front seat of this vehicle was a lifeless Ralph "Pecker" Romero, three bleeding holes in his head, face and shoulder.

The tree limb found its way wedged under our driver's side rear tire, and then I helped Joey and Sarah into the truck bed, on the same side. Hopefully it was enough.

Seeing that no one else was interested in us, I threw us back into gear, and nudged us off the flattened car and back onto pavement. I flipped us around so we'd pass by the new Range Rover. I slapped the side of the truck so that Sarah could see. In my rear view mirror, I saw her nod.

At least Pecker's vendetta had died with him.

Another set of headlights flashed in our direction. But that vehicle was just turning, and moved away from us. So I moved us to the other side of the property and waited, watching for our way to be clear and eyeing Sarah as she worked on Joey.

When there were no more vehicles coming down the road, I put us back into gear and we headed back home, sick from our defeat.

We'd just lost all of that food, and worse, we may have lost our new friend Joey. He would have been a valuable addition to our group. On the other hand, we'd killed a predator who was gunning for us. If Joey somehow made it through, losing the food would have been worth it.

I glanced in my rearview mirror before turning onto our main road and caught another glimpse of Sarah.

She was sitting up in the truck bed, crying.

Four Days Later

CHAPTER 26

Nan

It was the worst winter any of us could remember. And it was only May.

They said on the radio that global temperatures were down an average of over twenty degrees Fahrenheit. It had to be a lot more than that here, because yesterday the temperature never rose above freezing.

As a warm-weather person my whole life, I didn't even like visiting the mountains in winter, in spite of their beauty. At least they were white.

Instead, the heavens above continued to drop gray, putrid ash on us. Our silent killer. More than a foot so far. And none of us knew where this was coming from. Was it from one of the dozens of volcanoes around the world that had blown their tops or those in the Antarctic?

Where or why didn't matter. What it did to us was all that mattered.

And I received firsthand reports from Sarah and Ron, who would go out into it every day. They told me about the homes and commercial buildings whose roofs had collapsed. Or the stalled vehicles all over the streets. But the worst were their reports about the dead.

Sarah said some of it was from disease, from water contaminated by ash and sewage. But she also said some died from just breathing in too much of the ash. Ron said some of the death was from exposure to the cold and "other causes." I knew he meant murder, but he just didn't want to worry me.

Those who had survived the nearly two weeks since the wave hit didn't have it much better than the dead.

Stores were emptied long ago, and for many, their food had run out. Almost no one had stored food in their homes anymore, in spite of the lessons we should have all learned from the pandemic back in 2020.

Thankfully for all of us, Sarah was one of the rare few who had planned for this.

I would have been in the same place as everyone else, had I not found Ron and Sarah. And they continued to improve upon our situation.

Besides what Sarah and Bob had already accumulated, Ron identified other sources. He had done an inventory of homes and their missing owners in and around the neighborhood, and Sarah had keys to many of them.

So each day, Ron and Sarah would drive Sarah's Range Rover to the next home on the list and take their supplies—Ron called it 'repurposing'—if they weren't home. In every case, they'd leave a simple note:

"We've borrowed your supplies.

If you return, come see me.

B&S."

Ron had advised her to leave her full name off the note, so that it didn't lead to us if bad guys had broken in. And because few knew Bob's fate, Sarah signed as she and Bob often signed things.

So far no one, good or bad, had come to us to ask for their supplies back. And so our little family of misfits went about our business, so far without any outside interference.

Our family wasn't connected by blood, but it was as tight as any other, bound by a glue which was stronger than blood. We were connected by tragedy. Besides the daily suffering we mutually shared, each of us had lost someone close to us in our lives. It was this bond, and that of our unifying mission of self-preservation, that helped us work so well together.

After Ron and Sarah would return with a new load of supplies, they'd unload them downstairs and I'd inventory everything and recalculate our Food Consumption Supply Days or FCSD. We were up to an FCSD of 216 for all of us after the last load. That one was a gold mine, with lots of canned and bottled food, medicines, batteries, and so much more.

Unfortunately, it still wasn't anywhere near what we needed for long-term survival. But each time I brought it up, Ron would tell Sarah and me not to worry; he had a plan for the future. Of course, he wouldn't say what that was.

Like Ron, we each kept to ourselves most of the time, doing our duties.

I did the inventory and made breakfast and dinner. I wasn't a great cook, since I had only a few dishes in my repertoire. But everyone went to bed some time afterwards satisfied. Or they never said anything different.

Ron seemed tireless.

After he would return with Sarah from a supply run, he'd usually go next door with Dog, to his workshop. Most nights he'd stay there all night and return with Dog in the morning for breakfast.

Ron never told us what he was working on, only that he was 'building stuff.' He did have a knack for building things. But then he'd just announce each project after it was completed, all casual-like, as if it wasn't that important: "Hey, I built a water pump and filter system, pumping water from the river, so we won't die from drinking contaminated water—can you pass the bread?"

Or "I added filtration to our vehicles so that they won't choke to death on the ashfall, like every other vehicle on the planet—how was your day?"

When he was at Sarah's—our mutual home—he'd be reading some of Bob's prepper books. He did this every moment we saw him, other than when he was leaving or returning. When asked what he was reading, he'd never say... more secrets.

There was one exception to this pattern.

Last night, he'd stayed up reading and fell asleep in the armchair, with Dog curled up by his feet. When I tried to put a blanket over him while he was sleeping, Dog growled at me. I wasn't put out, though; he did this to anyone who tried to get in between him and Ron. It was as if he too were protecting his master and his master's secrets.

Regardless of the project, Ron always did it alone. He seemed to prefer doing things alone. It was as if he didn't like people very much, not even those who cared for him.

Some of this was surely because of the loss of his wife. Especially after Sarah sat him down and told him the story Phyllis had told us about what happened to Liz. From what I heard, he thanked Sarah calmly and never said another word about it.

Perhaps it was all just too much loss for one person, and he feared getting to feel too much for others, when there was a pretty good chance of their dying in this apocalyptic world. I could only guess.

My hope was that he was just too damned tired. I know I was.

Either way, I knew he needed time to process everything. He was like that with most things.

My radio chirped, almost as a reminder of the time. It was either Ron or Sarah checking in on me. I clicked the mic three times, our agreed upon signal to acknowledge that we were all right.

I clipped the unit to a belt loop on my pants, ladled some soup into a bowl and walked it carefully down the hallway, until I was standing before the study door.

Using the solid plaster cast on my right arm—another creation of Ron's—I rapped a couple of times and waited for a reply.

The groggy voice answered, and I opened the door.

"Good morning. How's our patient today?" I asked.

He worked up a smile.

I sat down beside him, on the edge of his makeshift bed.

The first spoonful was readied and Joey immediately responded, "That's amazing, ma'am. Thank you."

The approaching rumble set off my own panic and alarm bells.

Buster's men? I always thought.

Even with Pecker dead, we weren't one hundred percent sure that Buster and his men weren't still searching for us. Though after Bud got mauled, we felt pretty confident that they weren't too anxious to investigate Sarah's home anytime soon. After all, they were probably just as busy as us with their own home pillaging. It was all an unknown. And that was why we had to remain always vigilant.

I scooted up to the front door, my .357 in hand, and peeked into the eyepiece. The view was even more limited than before, as we kept the shutter down 24/7. Ron had made it at least usable by cutting out a hole with his welder, through which I could see anyone coming up from the street.

I smiled at what I saw, backed away and sauntered to the garage interior entry, with my radio now in my other hand.

It crackled on cue. "We're at the door, can you let us in?" Sarah called.

"Coming," I replied.

Since the incident with Bud—who may also have been dead for all I knew—whomever remained in the house would engage the garage door deadbolt, so that no one could enter from the outside.

I made my way into the garage, immediately feeling the cold. A quick yank at the bolt and that released it. Then I lowered the large loop of rope Ron had designed for me to make life easier. Placing this around my waist, I walked the garage door open, until it slid the rest of the way on its own.

Swirls of gray ash blew in, along with Sarah's Range Rover.

The driver's door popped open while the vehicle was still in motion, and Dog burst out.

I was ready for him this time.

He made like he was going to leap for me and I acted startled, but then ducked. Dog bounded at me, and then slid into me sideways, nearly knocking me down. I laughed and scratched his haunches and he woofed back with delightful enthusiasm. It was our way of greeting each other. He then ran back to his master.

Ron followed, hopping out and shooting me a strange look, like he did when he was holding back one of his secrets.

"Where's Sarah?" I belted out. She usually came out with Dog. "What happened?"

Ron said nothing, but nodded to the passenger door, or what was behind it. Then he opened it up.

Sarah hopped out, looking just fine. But before responding to me, she turned on a heel and returned her attention to the truck. "Come on, honey. It's okay," she coaxed someone or something from the inside.

A little dark-skinned girl, who couldn't have been more than nine, timidly hopped out. Her bare feet slapped the concrete and she looked up at me, her face pensive. Her arms, legs and face were carpeted in cuts and bruises. She looked as bad as I did after the earthquake... Still do, in fact.

"Here's our newest addition"—to our family, I completed her thought in my mind. "We don't know her name yet, but we know she's been through hell and back."

"Hi there." I smiled and waved effusively.

The little girl said nothing. She flashed her eyes up at me and then down to the ground. Everything about her was sober and demure.

Sarah put an arm around her and she shrank away. "It's okay, we'll look after you."

If we had known then why she looked the way she did, we would have been worried. Really, really worried.

CHAPTER 27

Ron

"I have bad news: No one's coming for you. You are on your own," blared the radio.

At the same time, Nanette shuffled into the kitchen, her mouth popping open, as if she wanted to say something.

I thrust out my palm to silence her, and without speaking, I pointed and nodded with a jerk of my head toward the food on the stove top. I had made breakfast this morning.

Nanette glanced there, holding her gaze at my propane camping stove, which we were now using instead of the non-functional stove. She nodded back at me, understanding instantly. Her face held no anger at my rudeness, accepting that I had a reason for being curt. She gazed at our newest addition, who hadn't said a peep since we found her beaten and bruised. "Morning Leticia," Nanette whispered and smiled, holding her hand out to touch Leticia's shoulder, then thought twice about it, and retracted before making contact.

Leticia once again didn't make a peep, but she smiled while she chewed away at her second helping of sausage and powdered eggs and gave a happy wave. The only reason we knew Leticia's name was because of her necklace. It was unique in that it had an infinity symbol on one side and the name "Leticia" stenciled in cursive on the other side. She had revealed it to us yesterday when we asked. Other than the map of abuse edged onto her face, and her rabid hunger, it was the sole piece of absolute information we had about her past.

We had found her wandering down a street, without shoes or socks, shoulders slumped, hacking up ash. She was so resigned to everything, she didn't acknowledge us. We had to stop in front of her to get her to halt and even register our existence. After some water and a few crackers, Sarah tried to coax her into our truck, if anything, just to get her off the street. But she wouldn't budge. Then Dog, who continues to baffle me with his intuitive senses, moaned a plea to Leticia and she entered, accepting his slobber-filled greetings...

I realized the radio station we were listening to had paused for way too long. And now I worried we had lost the signal or I had run down the battery after searching for a station for the last hour. Maybe the emergency radio needed to be cranked up again. Even the static was almost nonexistent.

I reached for the bright yellow radio I had placed in the middle of the kitchen table we all ate at. Its dial was almost unreadable under the pale light of a single gas lantern hanging from the inactive fixture above. Just before I touched the crank, it blared again.

"I repeat… This is KDPD Radio in Dallas, Texas. I'm using the generator for just the next few minutes to broadcast the limited news we have here. We will try to broadcast once per day at this same time."

My watch said it was just after nine.

There was another pause, but I could hear the loud crackle of static was being partially suppressed by the open transmission.

We leaned closer to it.

"How did you find—"

"Shhhh," both I and Leticia said simultaneously.

If that counted as speaking, that was Leticia's first word, I thought.

"The news so far is grim: An unrelenting ash cloud has covered most of the US and as far as I can tell, much of the world. Power is out in most places. Air traffic was halted long ago. Cars have been breaking down. The ash's abrasive properties are causing people to go blind, and more and more are dying from breathing in too much ash—it combines with moisture in your lungs to form a cement-like paste that you can literally drown in. Please wear protective eye and mouth coverings; even a piece of cloth will help.

"All social services have stopped: Our local hospitals have either closed or are turning the sick away. The police have disappeared, and the military is mostly non-existent…"

"Is this a recording?" Nanette whispered.

"Don't know," I said. "Sounds like—"

"If you've survived this long, holding out hope that someone is going to come and save you... I have bad news: No one's coming for you. You are on your own...I repeat... This is KDPD Radio in Dallas, Texas..."

I snapped the volume off.

"Guess that answers that," Nanette said and turned to Leticia. "Are you feeling better, Leticia?" She was obviously trying to change the subject, and I only then realized this was probably not the best thing to listen to with a battered young girl, who had suffered something horrible.

Leticia just shoveled more food into her mouth, her eyes darting around the table.

"She hasn't said a word," I said. "I found her in the kitchen when I got up an hour ago. So I whipped up something. She, Dog and I have been eating away, and trying to find out some info."

"Any luck?" Nanette asked, with her plate now full of food.

"Other than a few ham radio broadcasts, this was the only one I could find. And now you've heard that."

Nanette sat down with her plate. She looked as hungry as Leticia.

"I think the ashfall is causing problems with broadcasting, and we just can't hear them. That and the power outages."

Nanette took a bite and chewed on her food and what I had said. She covered her mouth with a hand. "Where's Sarah?" she asked, dropping her hand and working in another shovelful of food.

"Downstairs, I think. And Joey is sleeping.

"And now, since you're up, would you mind looking after our princess?" I motioned to Leticia.

I rose from the table. Both of their eyes followed me, their cheeks stuffed and grinding away with machine-like precision. When Nanette nodded, I turned to the door.

Each of us had our own pile of equipment in the living room, ready for our quick exit. We each had a heavy coat, scarf, breather-mask, goggles, heavy bug-out-bag, and weapon. I didn't need my pack, and only took my radio out, turning it on and clipping it to my belt. When I was ready to go, I yelled, "Come on, Dog."

A deep woof echoed through the house, and the monster-sized Mastiff leapt off the floor beside Leticia and bounded through the living room to my side, panting excitedly.

"Are you going to give him a name?" Nanette hollered from the kitchen, pausing her feeding frenzy to watch.

"Dog is his name," I said. Confirming this, Dog scratched at my knee with a giant paw. He was ready to go; he was always ready to go.

Nanette humphed and scooped some more food into her mouth.

"Ah, Nanette?"

She looked up, nodded, and then sat up from her chair and walked my way.

I had fixed the rolling shutter to work manually, and set up a manual bolt lock into the concrete. But the deal was it had to be secured from the inside.

A quick glance outside confirmed what I had thought. Even though it's less than 100 steps away to my house, we'd agreed to wear our masks and goggles while the ash was still falling. I slipped on Dog's doggie gas mask and cinched it down on him—he seemed used to it now —and then put on my own mask and goggles.

Looking back to see that Nanette was behind me, we slipped out the door, and then under the rolling shutter.

"Have a good day at the office, dear," she said.

I slid down the shutter and heard her secure the lock.

My workshop was as cold as death inside, even though I'd been using it regularly.

A push of a button started up a 2500 watt gas generator, its exhaust now going out the vent that had been letting in the below freezing temperatures.

Today, I needed my power tools. So I would use some of our precious gas on the generator.

Plus Dog and I need the heater, I thought as I rubbed my damaged albeit healing leg, which throbbed like a son-of-a-bitch because of the cold.

Dog grunted too, and I flipped on the switch in answer to both of our grumblings.

Seeing that I was going about my business, Dog decided to settle in. He plopped himself down on a rug, in front of the space heater.

My gaze remained on Dog, who had become my closest friend, accepting me completely. And yet I thought of what Nanette said.

No, I haven't named him, and I'm not sure I can... Yet.

"You don't need a name, do you, Dog?"

Dog ignored me. He knew I was wasting time, when I had work to do.

I had just one primary project that I'd work on today: power.

Sarah's generator was now fixed and properly protected so that no more ash would get inside. But I feared two issues: first was the gas we needed to power it, which was in short supply, and would only get worse over time. Second was the ash damage. Like our vehicles, I didn't believe the generator would last maybe a tenth of its normal life because of the abrasive qualities of the ash, eating away at its parts.

So we had to find an alternative method of power, and being so close to an always running river, that meant we could use it to generate energy.

"The question is, will you work?" I asked the cylindrical cage. Last night, I had welded it around my repurposed roof vent, which would act as my turbine. My hope was that I could drop this thing in the river and the cage would protect the turbine from debris, but still let enough water flow through and move the turbine, which would generate power.

I stuck a hand in the cage, and with one finger, I gave it a flick, and the turbine rotated around the axis with ease. A squirt of grease in each axis point and it was even smoother.

"This just might work," I said with a smile. "What do you think, D—"

Several pops from a rifle echoed up from the valley.

I flicked the generator off and we both listened.

Pop-pop-pop-pop-pop...

CHAPTER 28

Nan

"Five months! That's all the food we have with six mouths now to feed," I announced to everyone that next morning.

I'd screwed up the calculations. So I reran them and now I had to tell everyone the bad news.

After I made my announcement, they all looked up at me from the small kitchen table. Ron turned down KDPD Radio, which was broadcasting more bad news. I was panicked and I needed to hear what Ron's grand plan was and that it would be all right. I knew five months would go way too quickly.

"I thought you'd said our Food Consumption Supply Days were two-sixteen, more than seven months," Sarah asked, genuinely confused, but then she looked at Leticia, quietly eating and watching me.

"Besides there being six mouths, I found an error in my calculations. So I ran everything again, and I came up with an FCSD of one-forty-nine, not even five months. I'm sorry, but using the guiding info you and Ron gave me, I'm sure of these calculations."

"Then, it's settled," Ron grumbled, leaving his spoon in his empty dish. He scooted his chair from the table and walked to the living room. Our eyes followed.

Although abrupt, we all figured he was going to go next door and go to work to solve this problem, but on his own terms. But when he slung his BOB over his shoulder, we knew he was going out and we all stood up. Dog dashed from Leticia's constant petting under the table and parked himself by Ron's side.

Without waiting for the question, he answered, "I'm going to run some errands." He buckled his BOB's hip belt and reached for his gas mask and goggles.

"Is that really safe, especially in your truck?" Sarah asked.

I thought the same thing.

"No, but as Nan pointed out, we're going to have a problem in less than five months, and I have a solution. But I need supplies."

Of course he didn't tell anyone about his solution.

"I'm coming." Joey lurched forward with his cane.

"Thanks, Joey. But I think I'd rather go at this one alone."

No surprise there.

"That's not a smart idea," Sarah stated. "Son, at a minimum your arm and leg are broken, along with at least a couple of your ribs. Who knows how much cartilage damage you've sustained? And you're bruised from here till tomorrow."

It was too soon for Joey, but when I was in bad shape, I went with Sarah, at least to observe. "Maybe he'd be a good second set of eyes," I offered.

"Yes, Ron." Joey perked up, as he lumbered closer. "I can just as easily sit on my behind in the truck as you can... At a minimum, I can alert you if I see something you don't. My eyes are younger," he smiled. "And you know, I've got your back."

Ron let his shoulders drop. "Fine. I'll meet you out front. Make sure they lock the shutter." He didn't wait for a reply and slipped out the door, with Dog connected to his hip.

Sarah helped Joey with his equipment and locked him out.

If we had only known what was headed our way, we would have protested both their going.

Ron

"I'm going to build a greenhouse."

"Don't you need sunshine for that?" Joey asked. Dog's hindquarters were pressed against Joey and his face was in my lap.

"We'll make our own sun."

I watched his face contort, knowing this would happen, just like I'd known that this line of questioning was inevitable. I also knew what would have followed from the women had they heard the rest. It was why I didn't tell them. But Joey needed to know since I was bringing him back into the breach. But I didn't want to tell him everything.

Pulling the truck around to the back of my damaged warehouse, after making sure no one else was around, I coasted for a few yards just to look and listen. This wasn't the area in which I expected trouble: I figured this whole section had been picked clean.

I threw it into park. "I know you have questions. I'll answer them all after I get back. This is my warehouse. I'm going to grab a few things I need from it."

Joey bit his tongue, even though he was obviously desperate for answers. It was the reason why I wanted to do this alone. It always took longer to have to explain everything to someone.

"Stay here, Dog," I told him as he made like he prepared to spring. He groaned and then laid his mug back down on my warmed seat and I left the truck, rifle slung to my back.

There were only a few things that I knew the lumber yard, our third stop, wouldn't have. Since I did specialized machine work, I special-ordered most of my parts and had them delivered. And I had several heavy-duty batteries that we needed.

Luckily, these were still where I left them, untouched by the wave and Buster's gang of thieves.

The batteries and parts found their way into the truck fairly quickly, then just one last stop inside.

I wanted to confirm one thing: that my lockbox hadn't been opened; that it still contained my personalized papers. And some more items I hoped we didn't need.

Standing over the lockbox in the ground, I could see that the lock had been beat to hell, but had not been opened. I pulled out my key and the lock snapped open.

Glancing at everything, I could tell it had been left untouched. I knew my worries were stupid. As Nanette had pointed out, "Why would they be interested in your paperwork, when they could take whatever they wanted?"

I left the papers and gathered up the remaining ammunition I had left when I escaped in a hurry. I snapped in the padlock and hurried to the truck.

Dog was already sitting at attention, panting happily at my return.

"Here," I said, handing Joey the bag. "You'll find more ammo for the rifle and a couple of mags."

While I fired up the truck and took off, he confirmed my statement.

"All right, Ronald. While I load your additional mags, would you explain to me what you mean by 'we'll make our own sun,' and why you didn't want to tell any of us what your plan was?"

"I'll take you there and it will make sense."

Dog answered for Joey, groaning as he plopped his ample mug back in my lap. Both of them were impatient.

We turned onto the main drag, both of us looking around the perimeter for other vehicles and other people.

At the turn onto the access road, which led to the place Joey was almost killed, I slowed, navigated to the back corner of the property, and stopped. The two of them glared at me.

"Okay, fire away," I said.

"Three questions: Why are we here? What do you mean our own sun? And why didn't you tell the ladies?"

"I didn't want to answer these same questions from them, because I knew they'd resist my doing what I'm going to ask you to help me do. So it was easier just not to explain it. But it's another thing when the person asking is about to be put into risk because of my actions. So because of time, and you'll answer these questions yourself, I'd ask that you trust me and watch my back, but even that shouldn't be necessary because I'll be quick. And because it looks like this place is empty, I'd like to move right now. So are you in or out?"

I said all of this resolutely, but one of my hands was visibly shaking, belying my true nervousness about what I planned to do.

I gripped harder onto the steering wheel to hide this.

"I'm in!" Joey gruffed.

Dog yawned.

Upon hearing this, I put us into gear and maneuvered us to the back corner of Green Growers. But when Randell's warehouse came into view, I screeched us to a halt.

CHAPTER 29

Ron

"The whole thing is burned to the ground?" I huffed, disbelieving my eyesight.

"Well, I figured if we weren't going to get the stuff, neither would they," Joey answered my rhetorical question.

I found myself flipping my head from Joey and then to the smoldering heap that was once Randell's warehouse and back to Joey.

"... Mostly I figured they would be so busy dealing with the fire that you'd be able to get Sarah out."

I couldn't help but guffaw. "It definitely worked. But I've got to imagine Buster is pissed off about this."

"Perhaps, but his witnesses to the crime are dead, so perhaps he's taking it out on his own people?"

"Perhaps," I said and then lurched us a little forward into a spot between Green Growers and Randell's, so that the front and back of the properties were all visible from this one point.

"Okay boss, what's the plan?" Joey asked, while shifting to the other side of his seat, groaning just a little under his breath. He was obviously uncomfortable, but he wasn't about to say a peep.

The kid was only a lieutenant in the Army, but he had the wisdom and toughness of someone so much older. We were blessed to have him as part of our little band of misfits.

Dog let out a long groan, reminding both of us of his presence. As if we could forget about a hundred-pound drooling dog taking up residence in the front bench seat with both of us.

"Simple," I said. "I need you to watch for any unfriendlies. I'm going in and taking a few things."

Joey made a motion like someone smoking a joint, exaggerating his rolling his eyes in back of his head, like he were getting high.

I couldn't help but snicker. Humor was another trait I liked about this kid. "Hardly. But what makes Buster's marijuana crop grow indoors will also help us for the greenhouse project that I have planned."

Joey nodded, immediately understanding what I had intended. "Copy that, sir."

"Let's keep radio silence, unless you need to warn me."

"Copy. Do I have permission to shoot anyone, sir?" He exaggerated the motion of cycling a round into his 1911.

I knew he was half-joking: his way of showing his frustration at being physically unable to do much or his trying to keep things light for me. It did. "Not unless you have to."

I stepped out of the truck, tossing Joey one last glance.

Joey grinned and batted his eyes, while holding his pistol close to his face. Then he flicked on the pistol's safety.

Dog was sure I was going to tell him to stay once more, so he didn't lift his head from where I left it. His eyes were alert and expectant.

"Come on, Dog. I need all of your senses." I slapped my thigh, grunting at the pain, and Dog bounded up and out of the truck.

"Heel, boy," I commanded while eyeballing the solid-looking back door. I reached in behind my seat and grabbed my crowbar and tool bag. I was pretty confident about the getting in part, knowing exactly what stress points I needed to hit to break it open. It was the rest of the plan about which my doubts were growing.

A quick look around the property confirmed only a few parked vehicles... We were the only people in the parking lot.

I didn't even register the pickup truck we'd passed, now parked only a hundred yards behind us, with a man in the front seat smoking a doobie.

Nan

Pop-pop-pop!
More gun shots. Though they seemed pretty far in the distance, I had to check again.

I glared through the peephole, looking for any sign. Nothing!

The sound of gunfire was never a rarity out here, even in our more liberal, anti-gun slice of Texas. But over the past 24 hours, it had been constant: every ten minutes or so they would sound off in a different part of the valley. But they'd been getting closer.

It was as if a couple of groups were systematically shooting, then moving closer to us, shooting again, and then moving closer.

"It's nothing," I announced to Sarah, who was cleaning up in the kitchen and laying out food for the next meal: some sort of freeze-dried mystery meat and canned tomatoes. Sarah's canned veggies were to die for.

"What, dear?" she said, sticking her head in the doorway.

"Just wanted to let you know it was nothing... the last round of gunfire."

"Mmm. You know, with our shutters down, we're almost impregnable. That's why Bob chose the shutters we bought. They cost a bloody fortune, but turns out, like most of the things Bob planned for us, it was a great investment."

She was staring at the floor, lost in her own thoughts, as she often was when she mentioned her husband.

"When you're done there, would you meet Leticia and me downstairs? I have a new project for us, since the boys are out playing in their sandbox."

"Okay. I'll be right down."

Sarah moved out of the doorway, and I heard her step to the downstairs entrance and down the stairs, where her muffled voice had risen a few octaves. "Are you ready for a game, Leticia?"

I stepped away from the door, intending to go to my room and put on a fresh change of clothes. I felt only a little pain today, other than the constant itching from a couple of wounds still healing. I wanted to wear something that was sunny—even if it really wasn't outside. I was thinking we had a lot to celebrate, and so our attitudes and what we wore should show this, especially around Let—

Pop-pop-pop-pop-pop!

Those were really close.

I returned to the front door and pressed my eye to the peephole.

I blinked, disbelieving what I saw.

It was Bud.

He was still wearing a white T-shirt, but he was clutching his gut, which appeared to be red.

He'd been shot.

CHAPTER 30

Ron

G etting in was the easy part.
By the time I was inside, I was already having second thoughts and both hands were shaking worse. What made me think that breaking into a mob-owned marijuana growing operation made any sense whatsoever?

And how could I carry a crowbar, flashlight and my tool bag, while still having my rifle ready to shoot? Every man thinks of himself as a special ops soldier when carrying some of the gear, but only a rare few actually are. And that certainly wasn't me.

Dog was my equalizer. I had faith in him.

He would be my eyes and ears, since he could sense something long before I could. And if shit happened, and it always seemed to, he would protect me.

After rethinking my get-up, I figured the crowbar would make a better close-quarters weapon. So I moved it to my right hand and slung my rifle across my back, out of the way. With my flashlight in my other hand, pointed forward, I lifted up the tool bag from the polished tile in the reception area and made my way to the growing operations. Dog glued himself to my side, his ears perked up and hyper alert.

I had never been inside an actual pot farm, but I had seen videos. Purely from the process side of things, modern day growers had very slick operations. And yet I was quite surprised that Green Growers was every bit as slick as those in the videos. Perhaps more.

Knowing that Buster was involved, I had envisioned a more shoddy-looking facility, run by sleazy characters. But everything here was high-tech and top of the line.

The only reason I was sure that Buster was involved at all was because Buster's father, Hector "Polar Bear" Morales, was front and center in all the news coverage about this place. I remember Hector at the opening ceremony, shaking hands, a toothy smile shining from his bushy white mountain-man beard and substantial hair, while he sucked on a twenty-dollar cigar. And in the corner of the screen was his equally fat son, Roberto "Buster" Morales, also smiling wildly, probably because he knew he'd have free pot for life.

I held up at the first door, on which a large placard said, Administration Only: No One Past This Point.

A quick glance at Dog told me he sensed nothing on the other side.

In clumsy fashion, I clicked off the flashlight, plunging my world into darkness. I pulled the door open and listened before stepping inside.

Other than my rapid breathing and Dog's low pants, it was silent and there was not even the faintest trickle of light coming from anywhere. I still let my eyes adjust, looking from side to side and listening for the slightest sound. Dog was pressed hard against my side, either because he was also disoriented or he wanted me to know he was there. Probably the latter.

At once, two overwhelming feelings hit me: being in an endless space and a gut-twisting smell.

I had smoked pot a few times before as a kid, but never as an adult. So I'd forgotten what it smelled like. This was different: a combination of cat piss, turpentine and dead pine-needles. Not at all what I expected.

Finally, after being sure there was nothing else living inside, I flicked on my light.

"Wow!"

The feeling of endless space was dead on. This place was huge. Football stadium huge.

As far as my beam of light would travel, a forest of marijuana plants stretched into the distance. Only they were all dead.

Of course, I said to myself.

The power had been out for almost two weeks now, and like most plants, these wouldn't grow well in total darkness and without power to pump water and nutrients to them.

I pointed my beam skyward and spotted my targets: grow lights. A heaven full of them.

They were smaller than I thought. So I did a couple of quick calculations and figured a dozen of them should work well in our greenhouse, once it was built.

With my beam, I followed the grow lights' wiring up, through their brackets and the steel superstructure that covered the walls and ceiling of this building.

And I got to work, leaving Dog to stand guard.

It took an hour of shimmying up, snipping the wires, and lowering the grow lights down to the ground, before I had a dozen of them.

Tying them into two spaghetti bundles, I was able to hoist the whole load at once over both my shoulders.

Dog didn't say a peep the whole time, acting more tired than normal. And when I motioned for us to leave, he stumbled a little before getting out in front of me.

That should have been my first alarm that something was off with him. The second was when he found our exit door leading to reception. Or rather, when his head found the door.

Dog marched forward, licking his chops and drooling even more than he usually did. I figured it was thirst, as I was thirsty too, and damned hungry. But as Dog approached the door, rather than slowing down, and sitting and waiting for me to open it, he marched right into it like he was using his head as a bumper. Dog looked up, startled and then groaned. He shook his head, shooting spittle everywhere, and then sat in a heap.

I was experiencing some... disorientation too.

When I reached the same door, I had difficulty judging how to get out: the opening was smaller than I had remembered. But when I tried to figure out how to make this work, my head throbbed and I felt dizzy. It was as if the process of thinking was tasking my brain too much. I laid down my load and the room moved.

I glanced at Dog, who looked like he might fall over. And then it hit me. We were stoned.

Just breathing in the uncirculated air, heavy with the broken-down molecules of thousands of pot plants, was affecting both of us. We needed to get out of here.

I grabbed one spaghetti strand of lights, left my bag, and made it out the door, Dog lagging behind me.

Then into the reception area, the lines of the floor moving with each step until I reached the outside door and pushed it open.

I sucked in the outside air, not caring about my breathing in the falling ash.

It felt glorious.

Completely forgetting where I was for a moment, I opened my eyes and couldn't see my truck. It was gone.

The world around me danced a little and then held. Dog barked his joy.

Panicked, I snapped my head in the other direction and saw Joey. He'd moved the truck.

The taillights flashed and he drove over to me.

"Shit, you gave me a heart attack," I said into the crack in the passenger side window. I felt a fit of giggles burbling up, like I wanted to laugh uncontrollably.

"Sorry, Ronald. We had some company, so I moved the truck into a spot I thought would be harder to see. We're all clear now."

"Good," I said, then coughed like I was suffering TB.

My coughing spell lasted a good minute, but it actually was good. My head was still pounding, but I felt less lightheaded.

Dog coughed too, standing wobbly a few feet from me. He coughed again and then ralphed up spittle and ash and then looked at me like he wanted to ask, "What the hell did you do to me?" I sent him inside the cab.

After dropping the first load of lights into the truck bed, I went in for the second set and my tool bag. I wanted to drop off my rifle with Joey, but I had learned my lesson: Never go anywhere without your gun, especially when there's a potential threat around.

I wore my face mask in to get the second load, and in no time, I was back in my truck.

"You okay with me driving?" Joey asked.

"Are you good to drive?"

"I have to use my left foot, but otherwise, I'm good."

"Great. It's better anyway that you drive now. Let's get out of here then. My head is pounding and I need to close my eyes. Let me know if you need me."

Like a felled oak tree, Dog listed my way, putting all of his weight against me, and made a groan-yawn noise. He laid his head on my shoulder and I swore he blew raspberries at me. I'd never witnessed a stoned dog before now. I couldn't stop the feeling this time. I started to laugh.

It started as a snicker, and then grew into something uncontrollable. Joey glared at me like I was possessed, but I didn't care. That was, until a wave of nausea hit.

With that, I laid my pounding head back and closed my burning eyes, Dog's wet mug up against mine, blowing raspberries. And the laughing continued in spite of my nausea.

Was it any wonder that neither of us noticed our passing the white truck a second time, nor that it pulled out behind us and followed us out of the parking lot?

CHAPTER 31

Nan

Clang-clang-clang, he pounded with one balled fist on the shutter. His other was pressed against his belly as a red plume seemed to grow out from it.

He looked scared.

His pleas were muffled.

I clicked on the intercom to hear his words. They sounded tortured.

"...they think I double-crossed them... Please, I know you're there, Nan-baby. I knew it was you who told that dog to stop attacking me... I was so wrong, baby, to screw that little bitch. She's with Buster now... I know I deserve what's coming my way... I'm just asking you to please help me... Don't let me die out here... Alone."

He looked down at his hand, as he pulled it away from his stomach. "Oh God, it hurts, baby. They shot me in the gut. And now they're hunting me down, like a dog, for turning on them."

He snapped his head, and glanced behind and then returned his gaze to the opening in the shutter. "Oh God, they're almost here." He did sound panicked.

And behind him, in the distance, I could see a man walking in our direction.

Could he be telling the truth?

Could he have done the right thing and turned on his boss?

I scrutinized his face, his expression...

Was he crying?

I knew what I was about to do next was a huge mistake. But Christ, after nine years of marriage, as much as I didn't care for him, I couldn't let him die, on the one chance that he wasn't telling the truth.

I unbolted the front door and opened it.

Behind me was some sort of commotion, but I ignored it and focused on Bud.

He looked up and then down again. He was... sobbing? A man who I had never seen cry. Not once.

A quick glance at the other man who was fast approaching the house told me there was still time if I could pull Bud in immediately. So I unlatched the shutter deadbolt and yanked up the shutter.

Sarah's hollered something.

Bud stepped back a little to give me room. Then he looked up, still sobbing, and his expression changed in a flash. He wasn't sobbing after all...

He was laughing.

He pulled his hand away from his wound and I smelled it instantly.

Not blood. Catsup.

Behind the standing open door, I heard Sarah's frantic voice. "Stand back. Move back!"

I looked into Bud's eyes and I saw it. Something I didn't know existed in him. It was true evil.

Before I could step back, I caught a blur of him whipping a gun out from behind him. It arced in the air and came around, across my face, spinning me back to the door and sending me to the ground.

The rest was a fog.

Sarah and Leticia.

A gunshot.

Bud standing over me, smiling and then saying, "I'm going to make you pay for what you did to me."

I was kicked and men ran over me and into the house.

Screaming.

A shotgun blast.

I hoped Sarah killed them all.

That was it.

CHAPTER 32

Ron

"We've got company," I announced, glaring at the red glow in my side mirror, lagging behind us.

"It's a white pickup," Joey announced. "We passed him in the back parking lot—"

"Shit," I cut in. "I thought I saw a flash of light coming from inside the cab when I first went into the building. I figured it was just my nerves." I gulped back the nausea and pushed Dog more upright so I could turn and get a better look at it.

"Yeah, I missed him too. Suggestions?" Joey slowed us down at the turn-off from the access road.

I commanded my brain to think straight, but I felt like I was floating.

Enough of this!

I reached down and squeezed my leg, just above the wound, and received the desired shot of pain.

"He hasn't engaged us," I grunted. "So I'm thinking he wants to see where we go. Let's try and lose him."

We pulled up to the stop sign, the T in the main road providing us two choices.

"I don't know this town as well as you. Where?"

"We need to go to the lumber yard anyway. Take him away from our homes: Turn left and drive normal, for now."

We both eyed the approaching vehicle as it slowed down and then braked to a stop. Whoever it was, they weren't very good at tailing someone.

When we turned, the vehicle released its brakes and sped up. He didn't even stop at the T and turned in our direction, while maintaining his distance.

I saw the lumber yard coming up, and then our chance.

"Don't touch the brakes. Prepare to turn in the Quik Mart... Now!"

Joey leaned into the turn, but neither Dog nor I did. My head clanged into the door, sending more pain to my already-throbbing head. Dog slid across the bench seat and slammed into me with a grunt.

Our truck's back end slid toward the building. Joey overcorrected, and we slid the other way. He corrected again and hit the accelerator, knowing what to do.

"There," I said, pointing to a small alley access. If we could get there before the white truck turned, we might have evaded him.

I glanced back to see the truck. Dog laid his slobber-filled mug on my lap and grunted some more.

Joey jammed the accelerator as we raced down the back of the property.

And then something happened to our engine.

It sputtered, and then quit entirely.

We coasted.

I flashed a glance back again and saw the white truck make the turn.

"Shit, he saw us. Stop here."

We slid to a stop, and I popped out, while bringing my rifle around. I stepped to the back corner of the truck bed, and benched it there. I knew what I had to do.

The white truck gunned its engines upon seeing us and aimed right for us. He wasn't coming to make friends.

I aimed for him.

Unfortunately, my vision was still blurry and my head throbbed so bad, I couldn't keep him from dancing in my sights. But I had lots of bullets, and I knew I needed to stop him.

Flicking off the safety, I aimed for the windshield and fired a barrage of a dozen or so rounds.

The truck swerved to the right, and then to the left, and then crashed into a dumpster.

I almost couldn't believe I hit him.

But he was probably still alive and might come after us, so I ran toward the vehicle, keeping my gun pointed at him as I ran. I glanced beside me to see if Dog was there, and he wasn't. The poor stoned boy must have decided to sleep it off.

Within a few feet of the white pickup, I could see I didn't hit the windshield. But it was cracked from the impact. I couldn't see a thing inside the cab, as if it were smoggy, but inside.

Holding the pistol grip with my right hand, steadying it against my shoulder, I opened the driver's side door and stepped back.

A gray cloud of smoke billowed out, and I was immediately overwhelmed by the last thing I wanted to smell... Dope.

It cleared a bit and I could see that the driver had escaped out of the passenger side, because the cab was empty. I hoofed it around the back of the truck and found him.

A lanky older man, with a full beard of gray and red. His head was split open and he was stumbling, but he had a revolver pointed right at me. He had me dead to rights because my damned safety was on. "Wow, wait now." He pulled the hammer back and I flicked off the safety. "Tell me—"

Dog hit the man like a freight train, knocking him to the ground and sending his pistol flying.

He had the guy by the shooting arm and shook him wildly, causing screams of pain and terror.

"Out, Dog. Out!" And Dog let go of the man, who scurried away, holding his torn arm.

I knew I should have run after him, but I wanted to get moving.

"Good boy," I commended Dog, who yawned back his reply, as if he were bored.

Both trucks were dead, and I felt we would be too if I didn't get moving.

So I hoofed it at a trot to a truck rental place, only a few blocks away. It was owned by a friend of mine and was the same place I assumed we'd use for hauling supplies from Randell's, before it burned down. After borrowing a clean box truck and stopping for lumber at the lumber yard, I made it back to Joey and Dog in just under two hours.

Immediately, I could see there was a problem.

Joey was waving in rapid and long arcs, half in and half out of my dead truck, Dog barking through the back window.

I pulled up to him and hopped out and he hit me with it.

"I've been trying to reach the women on our radio"— he held it out to show me—"ever since you left, but nothing. Finally, I decided to listen to the other channels, especially the one that Nanette told us about... Ronald, they found Sarah's house.

"Some guy announced to his boss—don't know if that was Buster or not—and told him that, and I quote, 'we found the house with lots of supplies and women.'"

CHAPTER 33

Nan

I woke to the smell of old carpeting and cigarettes.

All at once, I was rocketed by ice-picks of pain.

My head felt like an overripe watermelon in the summer sun, and it was about to burst.

I cracked an eye open; the other was smooched into the vile carpet, and I was instantly disoriented by this completely unfamiliar place.

It was some sort of seedy office, with 1970s furniture and stacks of papers and a nauseating voice in the distance behind me. The glare of the overhead lights only added to my pulsating headache.

I lifted my face—it felt swollen—to get a better view, and to get away from the revolting carpet. I knew it was going to hurt.

There was no stopping my stomach-clenching grunt. As my head lifted, my cheek still remained stuck to the carpet. I pulled farther and whatever was stuck separated from my skin.

I didn't want to know.

Beep. "I'll call you back."

Pushing with my arm, and more grunts, I put more distance between me and the carpet. My chest was now singing to my regular orchestral choir of pain.

"Let the boss know she's awake." It was Bud's voice. I gulped back bile, and my sorrow. Sarah didn't get him and that could only mean...

I couldn't even think about it.

A door creaked open, and I turned to face Bud... And a man marching in, with Chloe shuffling behind him, wearing a painted-on dress, bright red lips and a partially covered bruise on her cheek. I was sure it must be Buster, the head of the group of degenerates who attacked us.

I couldn't help but stare at this man.

At least Bud was a somewhat handsome man, albeit rough. Buster, however, resembled a nightmare. This man looked as if he were beaten with an ugly stick every day of his life. And then to make himself more revolting, he tattooed the left side of his face with some unrecognizable doodle. I shot a glance past him at Chloe.

And now the little tart who banged my evil husband was with Buster. Some women like power over beauty, I thought. But even that thought hurt.

Chloe didn't even look at me, keeping her eyes glued to Buster's heels.

"So this is your ex-wife, Bud? You're not bad looking." He stooped over me, scrutinizing my face. "Well, you were good looking once, but your ex took care of that." He guffawed at this, as if pistol whipping a woman in the face was a humorous thing. I leapt for him, reaching out to scratch him with my only support. He stepped away, and I flopped back on the carpet hard enough to take my breath away.

"Oh, she's got spunk, I'll give her that.

"So to business, Nan. Who else do you have with you at that house you're staying at... that is, besides the two we killed?"

I sucked in another breath. No!

My eyes welled up, and I breathed out. "You bastard. I'm going to kill you myself..." I pushed up from the floor again. It was hard, but I was fueled by anger. "I'm going to—"

Something sharp jabbed me in the neck and I tried to react, but a giant hand clamped down hard on my shoulder and shoved me once more into the carpet.

I was instantly lightheaded. Then I understood that they had just jabbed me with a needle and gave me some sort of drug.

"Your choice," said Buster, now sounding farther away. "Maybe after several of our boys have had their turn raping you, you'll give us what we're asking."

I tried to react, but I couldn't even lift my head. And when I blinked, I saw double.

Someone grabbed my legs and yanked at me, and then dragged me across the carpet and out of the office. I saw Bud float past me, and then Buster, and even Chloe. She shot me just a glance, and I caught something strange on her face that I hadn't seen before in this cocky young woman. It was fear.

Out the door I went, unable to do anything about it.

Through a hallway, with the same course carpeting, which now burned at my back.

I turned a corner, into another office.

Being dragged across the door frame, I lifted my broken wing, to try and abate my entry. It worked for a second or two, but then the man dragging me just yanked harder, nearly shearing my arm off at the joint, and I was pulled through.

A face flashed before me that I recognized, but then it was gone and so was the memory.

I was hoisted up and onto what felt like a bed.

I didn't really hurt any more, and I didn't care.

I knew what was coming and I just wanted them to get it over with.

I closed my eyes and prayed for death to come first.

CHAPTER 34

Ron

Multiple, deep-set tire tracks told me what we had feared: We were too late.

Joey had my rifle at the ready, in the event one of Buster's vehicles appeared. We saw no headlights, except in the distance.

Still, we held onto a small thread of hope... Until we saw the open door.

I drove right up the dead lawn, carpeted by half a meter of volcanic ash, and jumped out, not even bothering to close the door or put on my gear. Dog was glued to my left side.

"Ash," Joey huffed.

When I turned around to see what he wanted and why he used my last name, I could see him struggle with the weapons and his crutch.

I rushed to him, to relieve him of my rifle.

"Go ahead. I'll be right behind," he said, as he began to hop toward the front door.

Inside, there were boot prints everywhere, and debris littering a trail which I knew weaved its way through the house to what was left of our supplies downstairs. My rifle barrel led Dog and me over that same path.

"You get downstairs."—I was startled to hear Joey had quietly pulled up to me—"I'll check the upstairs rooms and the garage," Joey whispered. "And don't hesitate. If it's not the women, shoot to kill."

I nodded and we split up. He turned into the hallway, and I entered the kitchen.

The table was overturned, the cabinets opened. It was like an apple that had been eaten to its core, and then discarded to waste away in the elements.

My heart sank further when I saw the blood.

A small splatter of blood along the floor, with droplets leading to the open entrance to downstairs. That meant someone was hit, but not too bad.

I stepped around the blood and followed its trail downstairs. At the top of the open stairwell entrance, I halted to look and listen. Dog sniffed and growled.

A flickering light from below led the way. No sounds but our breathing. I felt scratching in my nose and throat, but ignored them and headed down.

Each step down was excruciating, as I was sure I'd find one of the people I cared about hurt or worse.

The steps creaked more than I remembered, and Dog's nails clicked even louder. I sped up my pace, knowing that we'd already announced our presence.

Above, a door clanged open.

Then, movement just as my feet found the floor. I halted and held my breath. Dog halted at the foot of the stairs.

Below me, almost imperceptible among the tracked-in ash and broken glass, were more rivulets of blood, and bloody shoe prints—they were from a smaller person. The trail moved past the little table with the hanging lantern, which lit the expanse of this space, and continued into the first stand of shelves—now completely empty.

A crack of glass under foot, and a form appeared out of my right periphery. Dog growled.

I dropped to the floor as I swung my rifle around, just when a shotgun exploded, sending double-aught buckshot over my head.

I didn't hesitate, firing off four rounds in quick succession.

A small man, whom I didn't recognize, stumbled backwards, dropped a shotgun—Sarah's shotgun—and fell to the floor.

"Ronald, are you all right?" Joey called down from the head of the stairs.

"Yeah," I panted. "Sucker just missed me. But I didn't miss him." I stood over the man, just to make sure he was dead. His jaw was slacked open, his eyes vacant, his belly to his neck oozing blood. Dog sniffed him once, and quickly moved away.

"He's dead."

I was surprised I wasn't more disgusted by having to take someone's life. Just a week ago I was disturbed about having target practice on a corpse, and now it seemed killing came easier. Focus, Ronald, I told myself, and examined the shotgun.

"And he had Sarah's shotgun," I huffed.

"Copy. House is clear. Going to check the garage now."

"Going to make sure no one else is down here." I said this while scanning the large basement, made more vast by its emptiness.

My hope was now hanging by a thread, a thread I needed to pull at.

I stepped through the emptied shelves, no longer concerned about making a noise. I was sure no one was down here, as I knew Dog would growl. I walked a straight line to the very back of the basement.

It was obvious right away: The bookcase with Bob's collection of books was still in place, untouched.

"Dammit!" I yelled.

"Ronald..." a muffled plea called out above. "Get up here."

I ran past Dog, who turned and padded back up the stairs behind me. I crashed through the doorway, and turned toward the garage.

I could see Joey hovering over someone's feet in the garage. I didn't hear all that he announced.

Only "... is dead."

CHAPTER 35

Nan

"Just kill me," I moaned throughout my nightmare.

But no one would. Each man continued my torture, but kept me alive for more.

I didn't want to live through this. I couldn't stand the beatings, and the hands all over me, and passing out, only to wake to a continuation of this endless nightmare.

At some point I thought I had woken up again, although not from the next round of abuse, as I was in total darkness. This didn't make sense, because there was always a light on above a sink on the other side of the room.

But I had to be awake, because the room's putrid smells smacked me all at once.

This is what hell is like, without the heat.

And there were voices, very close.

Then I heard him and I cringed.

"That bitch shouldn't have left me; now look at her."

Laughter.

A bright flash of light hit me directly in my face, and then I realized why my world was dark: I couldn't open my eyes; they were swollen shut.

All my energy was focused on opening them... Then like a crack in a doorway, I could see out the slit of one eye.

I tried to use a hand to force my eyelids to open further, but my hands were bound above me to a bedpost. Even moving them slightly brought me more agony.

Bud stared at me, along with another man behind me.

I pleaded in a soft whisper, "Bud... help."

The other man just laughed, and then so did Bud.

And that was it.

Something deep inside me snapped.

I resolved at that moment that although I would certainly die and even welcomed it, if I could just take Bud with me I would have satisfaction. That's all I wanted.

This was not my husband. This was some evil demon who'd been making me believe a lie. And then to realize that he could just watch me suffer, and even laugh, while other men did unspeakable things to me...

I could not let him live. No, I would not let him live.

The other man moved away from Bud, opened a door. More cold breezes blew in, bristling my already frozen skin. I ignored it.

"I'll let you say your final goodbye," said the man before he exited, partially closing the door, leaving Bud to be alone with me.

His words told me I had little time left.

Good.

A plan came to mind.

"Bud... Honey, please untie me." I kept my words as soft as a whisper, though at that point, I could have yelled them. I fidgeted with my hands, knowing the movement would cause the cords to bite into the raw meat of my wrists. I moaned at the pain, even though that torment now brought me comfort. It added fuel to the fire that was already raging inside me.

"No chance, Nan-Baby," he said almost softly. "In fact, I'm afraid this is it for you."

"At least..." I croaked, "release my hands from the bedpost. One last favor, for old times."

I could see through my slit, he was thinking about it.

He pulled out his favorite switchblade, sprang it open, and sliced at the single cord that held my bound hands to the bedpost.

He turned away, to focus on closing his knife.

That's when I mustered all the strength I had left, and more. I leapt onto his back, throwing my tied wrists over his face and down to his neck. Then I yanked with all my might.

He hitched back, and then forward, like a wild horse trying to buck its rider.

Many years ago, a few kids in my high school class bet me I couldn't ride the nastiest horse in our county fair rodeo. I did, of course. The horse bucked as if his life depended on it. So did Bud.

He reared up on his hind legs, spun around to shake me off, but I pulled tighter with my reins, so that it dug into both our skin, burying my knees into his back.

He bucked again, and like the bucking horse in the rodeo, I knew I would not let go of my grasp on him until he gave up the fight.

Back then, my horse gave up and I had won, just like I did now.

Bud collapsed to the floor with me still bridling him. And yet still I held on, my muscles now spasming with cramps, blood spilling out onto the floor from both of our open wounds. Only I was panting.

Finally when I was sure, I let go.

Ron

I knew it was one of our own, the moment Joey yelled.

I just didn't know who, and I didn't want to know.

Still, as I marched into the garage, and my mind wrestled with the who, the trail of blood grew larger. Whoever this was, was shot and had dragged themselves all the way into the garage, losing a lot of blood in the process.

Upon entering, I could see Joey standing over the body, and although I couldn't see her, I knew instantly who it was. My heart sank.

Oh God, please not her, I mentally begged.

The wind whipped up outside, as if I was getting my reply directly from God.

It was Sarah.

Only, she wasn't dead. She was still breathing.

I rushed over to her.

Her chest rose almost imperceptibly with each breath. I gave a quick glance at her belly, and wished I hadn't. She was shredded... I was looking at an exit wound: They had shot her in the back.

I went through most of the stages of grief in an instant: shock, then disbelief, then sorrow, and then anger. I remained on anger, balling my fists and wanting to beat to death whoever did this with my bare hands.

"Ron... listen," she said, her voice soft and focused, like it was someone else speaking.

"Don't talk," I pleaded.

"Shhh... Don't worry. I'll be with Bob soon." She actually smiled. She must have been picturing him.

"Don't change..." her voice was fading. "Who you are. You're good... No revenge."

"But," I protested, "these bastards have to pay. They will pay for what they did."

"Nooo... Go, get Na... and Latic... Hurrrr... befo..."

She was gone.

CHAPTER 36

Nan

When I clicked the door closed, I was alone to deal with what I had just done.

I hadn't just killed any man; this man was my husband.

I stumbled over to his body and glared at his reddened face. His tongue—twice its normal size—stuck out, and his eyes bulged and were locked open. Those eyes which held so much evil in them were quieted.

By me, I thought resolutely.

I had no remorse about what I'd just done. In fact, I wasn't disturbed by it at all. Instead, I felt a sense of happiness at committing the act. At doing what had to be done. But I wasn't finished. And knowing that invigorated me even more.

I was ready to do it again. And then again. I wanted nothing more than to kill every last one of the vile bastards who had done, or allowed what was done to me. Bud was only the tip of this foul iceberg. I would dash it all to bits. Then I would be ready to die.

But my body had suffered too much abuse. I fell to my knees and every part of me shivered. Because of the torture inflicted to my body and the cold against my bare skin.

A part of me, the part that was the old Nan, wanted to curl up on the floor and just sob. To give up. To will myself to death, after doing what was necessary: killing Bud.

But that was the old Nan.

I pulled myself back up, realizing then I had grabbed the sink basin on the other side of my torture chamber. With both my hands still bound, I pushed myself above the basin and puked out my guts. It was mostly bile, so my already sore throat was made more raw. But I didn't care.

I glanced up through my slits and caught a glimpse of myself, and promptly bent back over and puked again.

That image in the mirror... That wasn't me. It was a monster. A monster that Bud and his men created. I looked again.

My swollen face was black, blue and red. A giant, zigzagging gash across my right cheek oozed. And my body... Oh my God.

It didn't matter, I told myself.

My body was no longer mine. They took that. What was left had only one purpose now: revenge.

Even though my senses were on overload, from the cold and all of the physical abuse I'd endured over uncountable hours, I was feeling stronger. At least strong enough to do what I needed to do next.

Back to Bud. I knelt down and gave him a push, flipping him over to get to his knife.

Deploying it easily, after seeing him do it a thousand times, I flipped it around and holding the handle, I sawed at the cords binding my hands. It was as dull as a butter knife—I was guessing Bud never sharpened it—but finally they came loose.

A few still clung to my flesh and those I had to pull off, each one coming off with a grunt and fresh pain and splatters of blood.

Then I found myself glaring at Bud's knife, almost hypnotized by it, and what this meant. I now had a weapon to use against these men. I might only get one, but it would be worth it, especially if I could get the right one. A satisfying image popped into my brain: Buster.

Later, I told myself, and folded the knife back into itself.

The next thing would hurt, but it was necessary.

I wobbled over to the wash basin, put the knife down, and turned on the faucets. Nothing.

Underneath was a half-filled water bottle.

I took a swig, rinsed my mouth, and spat out more nastiness. Then a couple of satisfying gulps and I instantly felt better. Now, the hard part.

At first I gingerly poured a few drops onto my wrists; each drop burned like acid. Then I just went for it. I didn't have all day. People needed to die, and they weren't going to wait for me to freshen up.

More important were my eyes. I poured some water in a hand and splashed this into my eyes. This actually felt good. Then I lightly rubbed some water into and around my lids... Not so good. Hot pokers came to my mind.

But slowly, as my eyes opened a little further, more of my vision returned. It was enough.

Next, clothes.

I didn't care about my nakedness at this point, after all that had been done to me. Besides, I entered the world naked; I sure didn't mind exiting it that way as well. But I knew I needed to give my body some warmth, if I were to expect it to perform what it had to do next. And it had been subjected to the cold of this room for too many hours.

In the corner, on the floor, I found my clothes. They were in tatters. But after a lot of effort, they covered most of my exposed skin and provided me some needed warmth. Yet it still wasn't enough.

A quick scan of the room and I noticed a jacket hanging on a hook on the back of the door. It was way too big for me and reeked of smoke, but it was warm and comforting, like an old blanket. I zipped it up and focused on my next issue.

Dropping back to my knees, I examined Bud for any other things I could use.

One thing I realized then, in this post-apocalyptic world where death was so common, was that unlike the movies when someone died cleanly, they always soiled themselves in real life. I remembered someone telling me, 'Life is dirty.' Well so was death.

It disgusted me the first couple of times when I witnessed it. Now it seemed like just a further confirmation of a factual occurrence, a natural part of death. I accepted this, just like I accepted my own fate, and plunged a hand in each of Bud's wet pockets and came up with keys, but nothing else worthwhile.

Turning him onto his other side yielded something wonderful.

A gun.

I drew it out of its holster and examined it with affection. It gave me comfort just holding it. But more so, it provided me a means of exacting my revenge on more than just one man. If I could just figure out how to use it.

It looked somewhat similar to the pistol Joey had, and not at all like the revolver Ron had given me. I searched my memory for the images which would tell me how to work it.

Nodding at a memory, I pulled back the top part of it —didn't Ron call this a slide?

A whole bullet jumped out and fell to the floor. I let go of the slide, and it snapped back.

This was how the bullets cycled into the gun, each time you pulled the trigger.

I looked around for where the bullets were held in the gun and found a button that released a long and heavy container of bullets. Examining it and the bullet I picked up from the floor, I could see how each went in.

Based on its size and the size of the bullet, I estimated it held ten bullets. That meant I could kill nine men and save the last one for me. I shoved the container back into the gun and it returned a satisfying click.

I'm ready.

I collected the knife—this went right into my front pocket—and Bud's keys, although I didn't know if they'd be useful, went into the other pocket.

I padded to the door, actually fine not having shoes on; shoes made too much noise anyway. I wanted stealth.

Taking in a breath—my last one from this putrid room—I glanced once more at Bud and gave him a piece of my mind. "I guess you should have left that bitch alone, huh bitch!"

Yeah, you're damned right. I smiled at that one.

With one hand I twisted the door knob, with the other I held my new weapon. When the door cracked open, I was assaulted by more rancid smells and the boisterous sounds of drunkenness.

A quick glance down the hall in each direction told me a lot. Both sides were lined with doors like mine, each with a number on it.

I'm in a hotel.

My mind directed me left, and so I did. My new gun pointed the way, with my finger on the trigger, ready to blast whomever appeared in front of me. Anyone who was in this place was part of those who abused me. So they all deserved the same punishment.

In spite of my feelings of strength earlier, each step felt difficult.

I had to get to killing quickly, before I ran out of what little energy I had left.

Just before I came to the end of the hall, I heard a noise. Like a footstep.

Before I could react, something hard struck the back of my head and once more I saw stars and blackness.

CHAPTER 37

Ron

Revenge possessed every fiber of my mind and body. Yes, I wanted to save Nanette and Leticia. But most of all, I wanted to make them pay for everything they did.

I'd never known hate before. Dislike, yes; disappointment, most of the time; distrust, always. Never hate, till now.

Sarah wanted me to do the right thing. But there was only one right thing to do with vermin like these, exterminate them all.

And this was logical, I had reasoned, because even if we could safely retrieve Nanette and Leticia, these people would never go away. They would always want more and they would take more, because there was no one to stop them.

It was up to us.

More than stopping them, they didn't deserve to live. They relinquished that right when they took Sarah's life. She was one of the kindest people I'd known. And the last person in this world I had trusted.

I would enjoy killing them all for what they'd done. Especially...

"Don't you think we should slow down?" Joey asked, "We'll be no good to them if we crash."

I glared at him for just a moment, for invading my mental multi-course meal of hate. Then I snapped back to reality. He was right.

I let off the Range Rover's accelerator, dropping us down below forty.

"Thanks," I said, and loosened my death grip from the steering wheel.

Sensing one of my hands would be free, Dog moaned for attention. And I reflexively rubbed his head. Achieving his goal, Dog promptly dropped his mug back into my lap.

"So have you thought about how we're going to storm Normandy?"

"Huh... ohhh... ah, no. I figured we'd just sneak up and into the property, and then we'd kill anything and anyone—other than Nanette and Leticia—that moved."

"So now you're a hit man, ready to take your revenge on Buster and his gang of thugs?"

"Damn Skippy!"

"Do you know right where the ladies are?"

"No, but I have an idea."

"Okay then. Other than having no ability to run, I'm ready."

He said this just as we pulled up to what the town called Potter's Field, an empty property next to Buster's seedy motel and attached warehouse. The only people who came down here were wildcat dumpers, and Buster's people.

We both fixed our gazes on the conflagration of buildings on top of the small hill in front of us.

From my understanding, Buster ran his base of operations out of this property: everything from prostitutes to gambling, stolen cars, and drugs. I was somewhat familiar with the property, not only because it made the news once, but because Buster had always insisted that I deliver his boats that I had worked on directly to him. Every other customer of mine picked up their boats at my shop.

I remember from one delivery seeing women and men coming and going from the back of the motel. This struck me as odd since I had not known this to be a working motel. Then a local news station ran a report on the suspected illicit activities occurring onsite, including prostitution. Equally odd was that the reporter who did the digging disappeared one day on her daily run, and was never seen again. The local sheriff, who we always suspected was on Buster's payroll, did nothing. And the story died.

It was time this man paid for his crimes.

Joey, Dog and I slowly trudged through an empty field covered in gray, as I described to Joey where we were headed. "Some call it The Castle, because the buildings sit up on a hill, and around it is a moat-like depression which gets flooded often. In between this moat and the buildings, and surrounding the buildings, is a ten-foot high chain link fence, topped with razor wire. There are only two ways through the fencing: the heavily guarded front gate, elevated to the street, and a small locked gate at the low-end back of the property, which provides them access to the river."

"And that's what the bolt cutters are for?" Joey grunted. He asked this in between one of the times he plunged his crutches into the ground with a slight groan. He looked in pain, but was as equally determined as me.

"Yep," I said.

I continued glancing at him, while adjusting the heavy bolt cutters under my arms in a small sack, and my rifle slung forward. Dog peeked at each of us through his strange-looking gas mask, snorting away at the filtered air. He looked like a dog version of Darth Vader. I would have normally found it humorous, but I couldn't imagine anything striking me as funny anymore.

Upon reaching the fence line, we could see we wouldn't need the cutters.

The northern side of the fence was a tangle of wire and debris from the wave. I had thought this might be, but there was no way to know. Some sides of the river were washed away, and others were mostly untouched. It all depended on how the wave had traveled.

"That makes our job easier," Joey huffed through his mask, out of breath. His goggles were pointed to the ground, in an effort to not trip his feet or crutches on the minefield of debris, all of which was obscured by the thick layer of gray ash.

We stopped at what used to be the fence line and took in the back side of the property below and to the left and the warehouse and all its bays directly in front of us. The buildings looked untouched by the wave damage.

"Was this place as... junky before the wave?"

"Yeah. Believe or not, this is an improvement. Too bad it didn't reach higher and wash away the rest of this blight."

"Copy that. Looks like our coast is clear, but..." Joey eyed the debris field in front of us, and his crutches.

It was obvious he wouldn't be able to navigate through all of the debris in his current state, short of crawling. Then I had a thought.

"How about I fireman-carry you up and over the debris, and then up to the warehouse?"

"Think you're going to have to, if you want me to join in the fun."

I had not done this before, only seen it performed. And I wasn't sure how my damaged leg would perform, even with an extra layer of bandages. But thankfully Joey was light enough and because we had left our packs in the truck, we crossed quickly.

I let him go at the top of the incline, where the giant warehouse began.

We removed our masks and goggles because the ash had stopped falling, and we didn't want them on inside, I slipped off Dog's mask, and we piled them under some construction materials. Our hands needed to be free.

To our amazement, we still hadn't seen a soul. More amazing, the back entrance, next to the closest of the warehouse bays, was wide open, beckoning us.

I looked at him and he at me, and after a nod, we walked in with our guns ready.

We gave ourselves a minute to let our eyes adjust to the even lower light inside. The only sources were the open door we entered through and another open bay door on the other side. The space was huge. And it was filled with a huge number of cars, lined up in each of the bays with loads of equipment to work on them. I knew a chop-shop when I saw one.

"They haven't been cutting up cars since their power went out," Joey said softly.

He was right, this part of the operation was definitely abandoned, as evidenced by an inch of ash covering everything. Except in the last bay.

Through the open bay door, it was obvious they'd cleaned out the vehicles to make room for supplies. Stacks and stacks of supplies. I suspected many of them were ours.

"Let's continue through to the motel," I whispered. Upon receiving a nod, I stepped through the least obstructed path. Dog and then Joey followed.

We stopped when two men surprised us with guns pointed right at us. Even Dog didn't warn us.

There was nothing we could do. Somehow, they had gotten the drop on us.

We lowered our weapons.

One of the two men was Tiny, the big Hawaiian who was with Pecker when I almost got caught at Sue Ellen's insurance office. "Who are you?" he asked. "And what are you doing here?"

Dog growled, but not at them.

Joey and I turned around to see three others with handguns approaching.

We walked into a trap.

I turned back to Tiny, who lifted his rifle to his shoulder and fired.

CHAPTER 38

Nan

Once more I woke to blackness... And gunfire.

Lots and lots of gunfire, but in the distance.

A door on the other side of the room burst open and in rushed a flood of air, smells and voices. Then the door slammed shut.

Heavy breathing... by more than one person.

A lantern was lit, casting a pale orange glow on that side of the room. It looked like a storage room, based on what I could make out from the shelves and stacks of boxes cluttering the place. I wondered how much of this stuff was ours.

"What, are we camping?" asked a voice I recognized instantly. My heart rate shot up and I felt around the floor for my pistol.

It was Buster.

I frantically felt around for the gun I'd been carrying and then remembered my getting struck on the head. Whoever did that probably took my gun, and left me in this storage area. But another thought occurred to me, and I reached for my pocket.

"No, sir. But the generator is out," replied another man I didn't immediately recognize, except my pulse shot up even more. The other man held up the lantern, bringing its light over to Buster and a demure woman who was beside him.

Her head darted from the light to the door. "Won't they see the li—"

Buster's hand whipped around, knocking her to the floor before she could finish her question.

That was Chloe.

He motioned in the air with a gaudy, gold-plated cannon in his other hand to the slight figure on the floor. "I told you to never speak, unless I tell you." He then turned to the man holding the lantern. "We need more men, not light. Besides, we don't want our attackers to know we're here."

I pulled out Bud's switchblade and flicked it open with a click. Then I focused on Buster.

"Did you hear that?" Buster asked, pointing in my direction.

The other man pointed his lantern, and also a gun, in my direction. He walked toward me.

My thought was to try and dart to them, before they recognized the threat, and take out Lantern Guy, then Buster. That thought passed when I couldn't even get up off the floor.

Hell, I could barely lift the knife very high. How could I disarm one man and kill another, even if I were in great health? It was certainly impossible when my abused body wouldn't let me do anything right now. As quietly as I could, I folded the knife back into itself, and slid it into my cast, ready for quick deployment. I'd wait for my moment. But right now I'd play the part of a feeble, beaten half-to-death woman. That was easy.

Lantern Man appeared above me, grabbed my uninjured arm and dragged me back to Buster.

I groaned, though not as loud as I wanted to.

"Lookie what I found. It's one of today's playthings," Lantern Man said, and in an instant I felt sick with the flood of images: this man was with Bud when they raided our house; he stepped over me at the door carrying some giant pistol; he pointed his pistol at Sarah when she was running away, and fired; this man was also one of the men who abused me, although he didn't rape me; he beat me so hard I lost consciousness.

My adrenaline was back in spades, and so was my rage.

"What's she doing here? I thought you said that you beat her to death," asked Buster.

I couldn't really see Buster or Lantern Man speaking, because he had me all twisted around when he dragged me to them. Now I was facing Chloe, who was only a foot from me. She reached over and touched my injured hand gently. And although there was little light, I could see that she mouthed, "I'm sorry." Tears leaked from her eyes.

She's a victim of these scumbags' abuse too, I thought.

The door burst open again. A man blew in, and promptly halted upon seeing Lantern Man, Buster and us two on the floor. He slammed the door shut.

Out of breath and slightly hysterical, the man said, "Boss, a group of men... From the house that Clyde"—

he motioned to Lantern Man—"and Bud found... The one with the Range Rover... are here... They're shooting up—"

"How do you know it's them?" Buster cut in.

"They parked their Range Rover in Potters Field and snuck in the back. There are many of them, and they're killing everyone.... I barely got away."

"I'll bet they're here for this one"—Lantern Man yanked my arm and lifted me up like a rag doll—"and that little black girl."

"Clyde, go get the girl and bring her back here. Pinkie," Buster said to the guy who'd just burst in with the story, "go bring me more men. We'll use them as bait and blast them all away when they come to us."

Both men left, leaving me alone with Chloe and Buster.

This may be my last chance.

I reached for the switchblade, which I had hastily hidden in my cast.

It wasn't there.

CHAPTER 39

Ron

The Hawaiian fired one shot after another.

His partner also fired from his rifle.

All of their shots were aimed past us.

Joey had fallen to the ground, spun and fired his 1911, before seeking cover behind a vehicle.

By the time I had sunk down, spun around and raised my rifle to shoot, the three men behind us were down and it was over.

I turned back around to Tiny and his friend. They'd lowered their weapons.

"But weren't those your men?" I asked, while raising myself up with the help of a workbench on one side and Dog on the other. Dog panted wildly, like he was invigorated from the whole episode. I only felt confusion.

"They were," said the Hawaiian, his face dropping. "But not any mo'." His features stiffened. "Boss gave the okay to murder people in their homes, and take their stuff to add to ours. The men were happy to do this. They were also ordered to kidnap women and girls; they'd be brought here for Boss and his men. I have no problem with whores or drugs; that's a choice. But all of this, it's wrong." He looked around to make sure no one else was coming.

"We had the chance to run away, and we were on our way out the back when you two showed up."

I was seeing red again, thinking about what Buster had authorized and what they were doing. "Have you seen a woman with short, blond hair and a little dark-skinned girl?"

"Yeah," the big Hawaiian nodded. "We'll show you where they might be."

The other man glared at him. "We were on our way out, remember?"

"You said it yourself. That we should do something 'bout it. Now there's four of us. Let's do something 'bout it!"

The Hawaiian's partner's shoulders sank and after a slight hesitation, he nodded. "Yeah, what the hell. If I'm going to die, it might as well be for something good. Let's get these bastards then. They call me Scar." He held out his hand.

"Ronald," I said and shook his, and then he offered it to Joey.

"Tiny," said the Hawaiian, who held up a giant mitt.

We all turned to a door behind Tiny and Scar when a little girl screamed from somewhere inside.

Tiny took off running, more of a fast-paced waddle, and we followed. We entered into what looked like a motel hallway.

At the other end, a large man appeared from a doorway, with Leticia under his arm. She was beating his arm with her fists, and she screamed again. And then they both disappeared into the farthest room, the door slamming behind them.

"That's one of the storage rooms," said Scar.

I started down the hallway, intending to do I don't know what, when Tiny's giant mitt clamped down onto my shoulder.

"Not so fast," Tiny said, "I've changed my mind."

Nan

When the door opened, and Ron was being led in by a huge Hawaiian with his gun on him, all my pent-up rage ebbed away, like blood flowing from a large open wound.

They walked right into the trap, and I did nothing to stop it.

When Ron saw me and his face tightened and turned bright red, my heart sank to its lowest depths.

I couldn't help but feel all hope was lost at that moment.

Clyde had just come in with Leticia under one arm, and now he held out his giant pistol in the other, pointed at Ron. Pinkie had what looked like a machine gun also pointed at Ron. And Buster held up his golden gun, hammer back.

"Good work, Tiny," Buster said. A stupid grin carpeted his pockmarked face.

Tiny didn't say anything.

"Where are the others?"

"Dead," Tiny answered.

Whatever energy I had in me was now gone. I could barely hold up my head and watch the inevitable.

Tiny looked around the room and then nudged Ron with his gun, and Ron trudged inside slowly, with his head down and shoulders hung low, his hands behind his back, like he was tied up. He looked utterly defeated.

"Wait," said Buster. "Is that you, Ash? You're the one who's been causing us so much trouble?" Buster took a step forward, now standing beside Clyde.

"Did you think you could march into my place and try and hurt me, and not pay the consequences?" Buster said this while slicing the air with his chrome revolver, like he were a teacher admonishing a petulant child for misbehaving in his class.

Ron said nothing. I expected some smartass retort, but he bit his tongue, and didn't even raise his head.

I thought about Dog, who never left Ron's side... Oh God, I hope he didn't get hurt too.

I was feeling so dizzy now, and what was left of my vision blurred to the point that I was seeing fuzzy doubles of everyone. Consciousness wasn't mine for long. A way out of this horror show. I didn't want to die silently, but I didn't have any other answers.

Then I caught just the slightest of movement from Chloe. She was still on the floor, but she had crawled over to a spot in between Clyde and Buster. And clutched in her hand was Bud's switchblade, opened up and ready to do damage.

Damn! I thought, as I gazed at her with newfound respect.

A grin grew on her face, and she swung the knife around toward Clyde's belly.

At the same time, Ron yelled, "Now!"

Ron

E veryone reacted in a flash.

When I yelled, "Now!" I grabbed Joey's 1911 from the small of my back, while Tiny fired his rifle over my shoulder. I heard Joey—who had my rifle—and Scar slide into the doorway, firing away.

I lifted my head and Joey's pistol at once, and took aim at the big guy holding Leticia, at the same time as a young blonde jammed what looked like a knife in the big guy's belly. He dropped Leticia and his gun and pulled out the skinny-bladed knife and ran for me.

I fired multiple times, appearing to miss him, as he rushed me holding the knife above his head. I caught a glimpse of Nanette wrapping herself around his leg, tripping him over, but he still plowed into me like a bus.

While gunfire blasted above us, I brought the heavy 1911 down on Big Guy's head with all my strength. This time I hit what I aimed for and he didn't move.

I heard yelling and then a weak scream, underneath the lead weight of the giant on top of me.

Tiny pulled the other big man off me, and I rose to see that Buster, although injured, was holding up a wobbly and absolutely wrecked-looking Nanette, a pistol to her head.

"Ash. Put your guns down, or I'll pop your girlfriend."

His finger was on the trigger of a large-framed revolver—a newish version of an old Colt '45 that Big

Guy had been holding—his finger pressed on the trigger.

"Okay," I said. I held the 1911 to my side and let it drop.

"And you two." I turned to see he was speaking to Joey and Tiny. Scar was down on the floor. I returned my gaze to Buster, who was the last one standing.

"I'm going to deal with you, Tiny, like I would any traitor. But you," he said to Nanette, "I'm done with you."

Several rapid booms, like explosions, filled the room. And I saw the pistol in Buster's hand discharge, as he released Nanette. I lunged forward, catching her as she fell to the ground, limp and lifeless.

I kept my gaze on Buster, who spun around to look behind him. And down.

Standing all of four-feet-nothing was little Leticia, with Buster's giant gold-plated gun in her tiny hands. She squeezed the trigger again, generating another large boom. Then again and again. Each shot blew away more of Buster, who finally lurched backward and flopped to the floor like an old sack of rice.

Leticia glared at the dead man, tears running down her face. She stepped over Buster's body, leaned over him and spat on his face.

Then as if snapping out of a trance, she dropped the gun on the ground, and ran to me and Nanette, throwing her arms around us.

"He killed them. I had to do it." She buried her face into my chest and sobbed.

CHAPTER 40

Leticia - Recording #1

M y parents and me were headed to Nirvana. A community that lived inside a missile silo seemed kind of silly to me at the time, because who would do that on purpose when there were perfectly good homes to live in? But what did I know then, other than that this community was started by a close friend of my father, who was also a scientist.

So my parents moved us from our home in Florida, in the middle of the night. We drove all day, with one planned stop at another friend's house, in the Hill Country of Texas.

We never made it.

Before we arrived in their friend's town, a giant wave had hit. Some would say we were lucky; my father would say he was only being precise.

You see, my father had known, to the minute, when we would arrive. Even with the abnormally high quantity of traffic, my father had been so focused on getting to their friend's house by a specific time. If he had been ahead of schedule... Well, I might not have made it here.

What happened next is fuzzy. It almost feels like a bad nightmare, where I forget what happened, but my heart is still beating hard and I'm out of breath... You know, like now.

I remember we were stopping for something. As always, father was driving the car and I was in back. I don't remember where mother was. But we were going to get back on the road to Nirvana. That's when we met Buster and his men. And they had my mother.

I don't want to describe in detail what happened, because it is just too awful... Buster killed my mother and my father. Shot them with his golden gun. And it was all my fault.

Then they took me to a place where women sell their sex for money. It was really smelly and disgusting looking. They said they didn't know what to do with me. So they took my shoes and socks—I believe they thought I wouldn't run away then—and locked me in a room.

My parents locked me in my room to make sure I did my homework. But I always did it fairly quickly, long before their stated deadline. And so I learned how to break out of my room, where I would read the books in my father's study. That was the extent of my roguish behavior.

Anyway, it was fairly easy to break out of that room, and everyone was busy with the women who sell themselves for sex.

Not long after that is when Ronald and Nanette found me. I was walking along the road, and I believe I had fallen into some sort of psychotic behavior, because I don't even remember what happened. Except several adults were very nice to me.

Then Buster's people shot and killed one of my new friends and I felt that burning feeling again. Like I wanted to scream and hurt someone.

They took Nanette and me once more to Buster's place.

I didn't do anything, but I waited.

My father taught me to always be patient. Scientists find solutions to problems by analyzing and patiently waiting for the solution to come.

I analyzed and waited, and then a solution presented itself.

Buster's big, golden gun dropped in front of me and I took it and did what he did to my mother and father. I fired that gun at Buster. I read in a novel that if you want to kill someone and get away with it, you should fire every bullet in the gun. That makes you look crazy.

But I was crazy with anger. The only thing I wanted was to hurt the man who hurt my mother and father.

And when it was over, I did what my father would never have approved. I spit on him.

Weeks Later

CHAPTER 41

Nan

Light... Dark—lots of dark... Then light again, with dark coming.

But this time, the light remained.

I knew very little: I was alive; I was awake; I was no longer in horrible pain.

What day it was or how many days had passed since the most horrible day in my life... I had no idea.

I also knew that over many days, I was visited by different people. Sometimes it was Ron—he would apologize and then move my legs and arms around; sometimes Joey—he would give me updates about what was going on, all in his wonderful drawl; sometimes it was even Chloe—that was damned weird the first time it happened.

But every day, Leticia visited.

Her first few visits, I was sure it was a dream because she was speaking words to me, and I knew that was impossible because she was mute. But after many days, I came to realize she could in fact talk and it was her words I was hearing. Obviously, some shock had caused her to not speak when we took her in.

Leticia was my little angel. Each time she asked how I was feeling. I'm not sure if I answered most times. But I remember this was followed by her telling me a story: A few were fictional tales or fables that sounded familiar; often they were elaborate fantasies, completely made up and originating from her own amazing young mind —she said she wanted to be a writer some day; and some of her stories were real-life, either all real or a combo of reality and fiction—I think she added the fiction to spare me any sense of hardship. Every day, I looked forward to Leticia's visit, finding I needed to hear her soft voice.

A few times I remember being woken by what sounded like a jackhammer. Loud reverberations under my bed made me first think earthquake, but the rumbles continued for several days.

I asked Joey what that was and he stated it was just Ronald, "doing his thang." But Ron never told him or anyone what he was doing, only that it was a project— one of many that he would one day explain to everyone, when it was ready.

Some time later, there was pounding outside, over multiple days.

Then Ron announced that the greenhouse was done. I didn't know what he meant by that. Perhaps it was one of the projects Joey mentioned. Ron was definitely excited by this one.

Then the day came when I could get out of bed.

Leticia arrived at my bedside, grinning ear to ear.

She took my hand and in the other she had a yellow device, which looked both familiar and new at the same time. She pushed a little green button and her beautiful voice came through the single speaker. "I'm supposed to help you, on account of you haven't walked in a while, and your legs have atrophied."

She clicked the same button, and slid the device into a purse she wore across her shoulder.

My mind swam. Had Leticia actually spoken to me all this time or was it a recording? I looked at her face. It was both dark and whimsical at the same time. She glanced at me; a little smile curled up into her thin lips.

With both her hands she softly clutched one of mine and tugged, ever so lightly, and I stood.

Another strange feeling: I was physically strong, but my legs wouldn't work the way I wanted. And oh my God, they were so skinny. They looked like two little matchsticks.

Talk about slow going. Leticia patiently led me through the hallway and then the kitchen, and to the back door. I was sweating, even though I knew it was cold in the house.

It occurred to me that I wasn't hearing or seeing anyone.

We stood there for a moment at the back door, Leticia allowing me to catch my breath—I knew that sounded crazy because I had barely walked thirty feet—and I felt her moving. No, vibrating. A bubbling cauldron of excitement, about to boil over.

I looked down and she was radiating sunshine, her bright, shiny teeth fully exposed, and she was literally hopping up and down. She couldn't wait to show me what was behind the door.

"Okay," I said, "what is the big surprise?"

She twisted the door handle with her free hand—her other clasped my shoulder blade—and pulled. I think I heard her whisper, "Behold!"

I stared dumbfounded directly into a giant greenhouse, which didn't exist days before. I snapped my head left and right, to confirm that the kitchen we had just walked through and the door leading to the garage were all in their rightful places. Then I returned my gaze to this magical place, and my senses were overwhelmed.

Fresh lumber, dirt and manure scents filled the air.

The walls were a translucent white, with dark shadings, like sand dunes, which flowed almost halfway up in some places, and then down. The shell was all two-by-fours. Bright lights hung from the rafters, shining what felt like sunlight above rows upon rows of dirt mounds, which stretched out from one end to the other. And each long mound had dozens of little green sprouts.

"Isn't it cool?" said Chloe, who didn't look like herself without makeup and her dirty-blond hair cut in a short bob, with bangs, just like I had worn mine. And she wore boy's clothes.

All I could do was smile at these surreal images floating before me.

"Our Chloe was raised on a farm," said Joey with a wide smile. "Farmer Chloe."

Chloe punched him on the arm and then gave him a peck on the lips.

Was I asleep for a year? I wondered.

Even Dog was there, digging in a dirt pile in the far corner.

I realized then it was warm inside, really warm. Heaters, which were spread around the huge space, glowed.

"But where's the power coming from?" I wondered out loud, not really expecting an answer.

"That's all Ronald," said Joey. He and Chloe were holding hands and staring at me, grinning, I could only assume at my reaction to this amazing place.

"What?" I asked.

"We all pitched in," Ron said, beside me, and I jumped a little at this, not knowing he was there.

"Sorry to startle," he said with a smile.

"No, it's just... So amazing. Are you using the gas generator?"

"Yes and no," Ron said, smiling with pride. "The energy is mostly coming from the river below. I rigged a turbine to run constantly to power a rack of batteries in the garage.

"We sometimes turn on the generator, but only when we have heavy power needs."

I couldn't think of what to say. My head was swimming and I was feeling physically fatigued, while emotionally overjoyed.

"How are you feeling?" Ron asked.

"Like I got run over by a fleet of Mac trucks."

"Do you need to sit down?"

"She'll be fine," added Leticia.

"It's like I've stepped into another dimension." I looked at the greenhouse and Chloe and Joey, and then at Leticia.

"Yeah," Ron said, "a lot has changed and you've been out for a while."

"How long?" I asked, thinking a few days.

Ron hesitated. "Over a month."

I felt like I might pass out, and I guess I looked it too, because he added his hand to Leticia's to support my back.

"Seriously, a month?"

"You were in pretty bad shape when we found you—"

I stiffened up, as all of the horrible images flooded back. "What about—"

"All dead. You're safe now," Ron said.

"We thought we'd lost you, you were in such bad shape. But it looks like you've healed well physically. The mental stuff will take a while. But you need to give yourself time."

Leticia yanked on my arm. "What honey?" I asked.

She was vibrating again. "You have to see this." It was her actual sweet voice and not a recording.

I didn't want to leave, but she pulled me back into the house, through the kitchen to the front door.

"Maybe when you're feeling better, we can have a snowball fight?"

Again, I was sure I was losing it, until she opened the front door.

Everything, and I mean everything, was snow white.

CHAPTER 42

Ron - The Next Day

And for the first time since all of this began, the sky opened up and spilled a little sunshine all over us.

By my count, it had been over three months since volcanoes filled our skies with billions of cubic feet of ash and dirt.

We had thought... Okay, more like we hoped, that we had turned a corner, and that maybe it wouldn't get any cooler. And even start to warm up in the foreseeable future. Of course it was a ridiculous thought, but what did any of us know back then?

Besides, seeing the sun, even if it were for a short time, was a moment to celebrate: We'd all been through so much, lost so much to get to this point, and we had come out on the other side, not whole, but in many ways stronger than we were before.

So we decided, as our treat, that we'd venture away from the house. Surely it would be safe to do so.

The two lovebirds shoveled a path through the snow and ash to the street. Then we all piled into the Range Rover.

We abandoned our masks and goggles, because there was no more ash in the air. Even the sulfur smell was gone.

We got to fully test out the snow-chains I had made, and they worked great. We drove slowly through the neighborhood, or what was left of it, marveling at what we saw.

Clearly, more than half of all the homes' roofs had collapsed, others had burned down, others were abandoned with windows and doors opened. Not one looked lived in.

Perhaps it was the sunlight, which reminded me of the "old neighborhood" as a kid, and how I played all around this area, long before there were much more than ours and Bob and Sarah's homes.

The whole time, I didn't tell them where I was taking them: It was a surprise.

At the final turn, we were at the very top of the highest hill, overlooking the entire valley, with views all the way down to Corpus Christi.

It was one of Liz's and my favorite spots, and we had sometimes taken a bottle of wine and parked up here, and spent much of the night necking and talking about what our life together would look like.

"Wow, Ronald. This is amazing!" said Joey.

"I wanna see," begged Leticia from the middle of the back seat.

Joey popped out from one side, and Chloe from the other.

"It's not the beach I promised," I said to Nanette.

"I guess it'll have to do." She rolled her eyes, feigning boredom.

Dog barked his excitement. He was anxious to get out too.

"Come on," I said.

Leticia was making and throwing snowballs at Joey, and Joey at her. Chloe just laughed till she cried.

I grabbed Nanette's hand, making sure she was steady, and led her to the lookout point. I sat her down on the edge of a waist-high wall that was a lot higher before the ash and snow had fallen.

I sat beside her and together, we admired the view.

"Pretty amazing, Mr. Ash."

She was right.

I took in a gulp of the frigid air, relishing its crisp bite, and gawked at the white valley below us. It was covered in snow, as far as our eyes could see, like some scene in the dead of winter in the Alps, complete with an S-shaped river cutting the valley in two.

The whole world looked... frozen. We now live in a Frozen World, I thought.

I felt a little hand grab mine and squeeze tight. That was Leticia. She smiled up at me.

"Isn't it pretty?" I asked and squeezed back. She nodded.

Someone grabbed my other hand. It was Nanette. "Yes, it is pretty." She smiled.

I marveled at how her wounds had healed, almost completely. She had only the smallest of scars across her cheek, which today she covered with makeup. Then I realized it was the first time I had seen her wear makeup since the day I met her. She looked pretty. Very pretty.

Then her face turned serious.

"Are we going to be safe?" asked Nanette.

I looked over to Leticia, fearful of where our conversation would go. The little body with a wise soul shot me a knowing smile, released my hand and then made squawking noises like a predator bird, and raced toward Joey and Chloe on the opposite side of the wall.

As I looked back at Nanette, she continued, her voice lower to make sure she wasn't heard by anyone other than me. "I mean, none of Buster's men are coming after us, right?"

I placed my other hand on hers and gave her a comforting squeeze and a reassuring smile.

"No, we killed them all. Tiny, who helped us kill them, was the only one who survived from his gang, and he left shortly after we came back. We took back all of our food and some of theirs, including some of their weapons. And we made sure that there was nothing left to tie us to Buster or that place."

She twisted her head, obviously confused.

"Well..." I hesitated, hating that I even mentioned this point. "You see, Buster wasn't the top dog of his crime family. That title belongs to his father. I have a feeling that dear old dad put Buster out here, where he'd do the least amount of damage to the family business. And when he got into trouble, mafia dad would buy his freedom."

Nanette's mouth dropped open and she nodded. "I remember now. I saw him on TV, after Buster's place was busted for prostitution—"

"Suspected prostitution. But all of the witnesses disappeared and Sheriff Wilkey pushed the rest of Buster's dust under the rug, and Buster was let free.

That one, though, required the great Polar Bear to show himself in public again."

"Yeah, the guy who looked like Grizzly Adams."

I was surprised Nanette even knew who that was, suspecting it was before her time.

I nodded.

Her face turned grim, as I could see she was thinking about how it could affect us.

"Not to worry. That whole mess is over now. And as I said, there is nothing of ours to tie us to what happened with Buster. It's all good."

"You'll keep us safe, right Ronald?" asked Leticia, behind me. I wondered how long she was there.

I picked her up and hoisted her onto a place between both of us. "Yes, I will. I promise."

We looked out silently over the valley and at our newly frozen world.

We were safe at that moment. We were growing our own food, using the heirloom seeds that Bob had provided—his best gift yet. And in a few months, it would provide us with fruit and vegetables to supplement what we had. We figured we could make it for several years now. We had water and power.

We should get through this fine. The only question was how long it would be before it got warm again.

But that was a worry for another day.

Off to the right a reflective glint caught my eye. And then there were two. It was a column of military Humvees, in the distance, coming from Austin.

I looked around to see if anyone else was looking in that direction, but they were full of joyful laughter and conversation.

The column continued its movement toward us and then it turned. It moved up the road toward Buster's property.

I opened my mouth to say something, but I didn't. It was a good day and I didn't want to spoil it. But my old friend anxiety started its familiar hold.

ENTRANCE INTERVIEW - PART 1
SUBJECTS: R. Ash, N. Thompson & L. Brown

EPILOGUE

Interrogation of Silas "Trout" Guzman - Recording
#124

Yeah, we pulled up in Oso Polar's four Humvees, to track down his son, Roberto.

Mine was the first Humvee to the open gate. The place looked abandoned, until I saw a body.

We didn't slow; we don't slow for no one.

We stopped in front of the entrance of what I can say looked like one of the shitty motels you'd find off the Northwest Highway in Dallas, by one of OP's strip joints. No, this one was much worse.

I'd heard stories about OP's boy: that he used too much of OP's product, that he liked his hookers too young, but mostly that he was insane. I could only imagine someone insane living here, even after the world ended, when he could have taken any of the other homes in this area.

"Trout, you enter with Ice and give us a sit-rep."

"Copy OP."

Ice took three others and did just that, finding the place empty, except for the dead bodies, each riddled with various caliber bullet holes.

Then we found Roberto, toes up.

I kind of expected this, because we'd lost contact with him for over a month. But what I didn't expect was how bad he looked.

The frost had kept him from bloating too bad. Still, it was almost hard to recognize him. And his stomach and pelvis had been shredded by many shots from a large caliber weapon. It looked like a revenge killing. I've seen many of those.

I couldn't tell any of this to OP over the radio. He preferred his news delivered face-to-face, "like a man," he'd tell his people.

Everyone knew this was so he could decide whether to kill you where you stood, with his giant claw-knife. Imagine how I felt, knowing I was the poor SOB who was about to tell him that his only son was killed. And there weren't nobody I could scuff it off to: OP was expecting me to report the news.

But I also knew how to deliver a message, so as to divert his rage away from me. And I knew never to use the son's nickname, Buster—he hated that name.

Even as trusted as I was, I knew one day I wouldn't escape his rage. Perhaps it would be today.

As I exited the building and approached him, I studied Hector "Polar Bear" Morales—most called him El Oso Polar or just OP—sitting in his Humvee. Upon seeing me he hopped out and watched me, his black eyes drilling into mine, looking for the answer I did not want to give him.

He wore his signature all-white parka. With his white hair and beard, in this new Ice Age, he fit his moniker more than at any point I'd ever known. He was a polar bear in this environment, like he was born for this time.

"Sir," I said, when I stepped up to him, facing him directly, and readying myself.

"Report, Trout."

"I found Roberto, dead from multiple gunshot wounds, and I think I know the motive."

I paused only for a second to check his eyes and facial features, to see if I needed to quickly get out of his way, or continue. He didn't even twitch.

"It appears he was killed for revenge. He was struck at least five times at point-blank range, and they were centered around his stomach and pelvis. Knowing his history with young hookers, this indicates a desire to get him where it counted.

"And because the shots were directed upward, I'm guessing it was a very small woman, or maybe even a child. Though it could have been done from the floor as well.

"Ice and the others are inside, currently combing the place for clues as to what happened and who may have done this."

Again OP said nothing, but his hand went to the scythe by his side, and I watched his face grow tauter by the second. I knew he would strike at any second, and I knew I would be the focus of his wrath.

If only someone else were here instead of me.

"Sir," called out Ice from the shitty motel entrance. He rushed in our direction carrying what looked like a map.

I saw momentary salvation.

"I found something you should look at." Ice walked over to OP's Humvee hood, opened up the map he'd been holding, and spread it out wide.

"It looks like Buster's men had been going house-to-house, and taking supplies from each. We found a bunch of supplies spread out over several of the rooms and in a big warehouse/garage out back. Though it did look like a large amount of supplies had been taken from the warehouse too. As if they'd been reclaimed by the person that Buster's men took them from."

I could see that every time Ice referred to Roberto as Buster, OP's face turned a deeper shade of red. He was getting pissed.

I quietly stepped back one step and then another, relishing the upcoming moment, even though I kind of liked Ice.

"This map is of the entire valley, and it shows dozens of areas highlighted in yellow. We're guessing these were the targeted areas: probably neighborhoods, full of houses. Those areas which had been cleared had red X's through them." Ice pointed to examples of each.

"You see there are only three yellowed areas left. But this area"—he tapped one of the three that had a red circle around a cul-de-sac—"is the only one with a red circle around it.

"My guess is that you'll find Buster's killer here, or at least all of the supplies that were taken—"

The move was so swift, I only caught the glint from OP's scythe slicing through the air. It was a damned good thing I'd stepped back, out of the path of the long arc.

Ice choked once, and grasped at his split-open throat, as he turned to face OP and me. A gusher of blood poured out from between his fingers. His eyes wide and questioning: What just happened and why?

"I told you..." OP stated, as he systematically sheathed his bloody scepter and then looked back at him, "I never want anyone to use Roberto's nickname again."

Ice fell over, like a bag of red laundry. Dead.

"Trout," OP turned to me, a splash of red coursing down his otherwise pristine white garb. "Find a place for me and the rest of your men and then tomorrow, you will take your best men to hunt down my son's killer."

**To be continued in
ASHFALL APOCALYPSE
Book 2**

Did you like Ashfall?

Help spread the word about this book by posting a quick review on Amazon and Goodreads.

Reviews are vital to indie authors like me. If you liked this book, I would really appreciate your review.

Thank you!

Want a free USA Today Bestseller?

As my way of thanking you for reading Ashfall, I'd like to send you my USA Today Bestselling short story absolutely free. Additionally, you'll begin to receive my Apocalyptic Updates each month, with information about my next release. There's no obligation to do

anything else and you can unsubscribe at any time. Just click on the link below and tell me where to send it.
https://www.subscribepage.com/ashfall1

Who is ML Banner?

Michael "ML" Banner is an award winning,
USA Today Bestselling author of Apocalyptic Thrillers

Michael writes what he loves to read: apocalyptic thrillers, which thrust regular people into extraordinary circumstances, where their actions may determine not only their own fate, but that of the world. His work is traditionally published and self-published.

Often his thrillers are set in far-flung places, as Michael uses his experiences from visiting other countries— some multiple times—over the years. The picture was from a transatlantic cruise that became the foreground of his award-winning MADNESS Series.

When not writing his next book, you might find Michael (and his wife) traveling abroad or reading a Kindle, with his toes in the water (name of his publishing company), of a beach on the Sea of Cortez (Mexico).

Want more from M.L. Banner?

Receive FREE books & Apocalyptic Updates - A monthly publication highlighting discounted books, cool science/discoveries, new releases, reviews, and more

MLBanner.com

Connect with M.L. Banner

Keep in contact – I would love to hear from you!

- Email: michael@mlbanner.com
- Facebook: facebook.com/authormlbanner
- Twitter: @ml_banner

Books by M.L. Banner

For a complete list of Michael's current and upcoming books: MLBanner.com/books/

ASHFALL APOCALYPSE

Book 1

A world-wide apocalypse has just begun.

Book 2

As temps plummet, a new foe seeks revenge.

Book 3

Sometimes the best plan is to run. But where?

MADNESS CHRONICLES

MADNESS (01)

A parasitic infection causes mammals to attack.

PARASITIC (02)

The parasitic infection doesn't just affect animals.

SYMPTOMATIC (03)

When your loved one becomes symptomatic, what do you do?

The Final Outbreak (Books 1 - 3)

The end is coming. It's closer than you think. And it's real.

HIGHWAY SERIES

True Enemy (Short)

An unlikely hero finds his true enemy.

(Get this USA Today Bestselling short only on mlbanner.com)

Highway (01)

A terrorist attack forces siblings onto a highway, and an impossible journey home.

Endurance (02)

Enduring what comes next will take everything they've got, and more.

Resistance (03)

Coming Soon

STONE AGE SERIES

Stone Age (01)

The next big solar event separates family and friends, and begins a new Stone Age.

Desolation (02)

To survive the coming desolation will require new friendships.

Max's Epoch (Stone Age Short)

Max wasn't born a prepper, he was forged into one.

(This short is exclusively available on MLBanner.com)

Hell's Requiem (03)

One man struggles to survive and find his way to a scientific sanctuary.

Time Slip (Stand Alone)

The time slip was his accident; can he use it to save the one he loves?

Cicada (04)

The scientific community of Cicada may be the world's only hope,

or it may lead to the end of everything.

Made in United States
North Haven, CT
30 October 2023

43408660R00157